She was about to turn off her phone when a text arrived.

I'm interested in you.

It was scary how much his admission filled her with a warm, giddy feeling.

You're a nice guy. I have fun with you. But we both know this isn't going anywhere.

She paused a moment before typing a bit more. I can't see you anymore.

Unexpectedly, tears formed in her eyes and she had to blink several times to keep them at bay.

Her heart leaped when the phone finally dinged again.

Have a good night, Sloane.

And just like that her heart sank all the way to her feet. Her hands actually shook as she typed, You too. And good luck tomorrow night.

Thanks.

She waited way too long to see if he sent any more messages. But none came.

Dear Reader,

It's hard to believe that *Her Texas Rodeo Cowboy* is the sixteenth story I've set in my fictional town of Blue Falls, Texas. When I wrote the initial Teagues of Texas trilogy, I had no idea the town and its inhabitants would continue to grow for years to come. But I'm glad it has. Blue Falls is as real in my mind now as many places I've visited in the real world.

In this story, another of the adopted Hartley siblings finds an unexpected love. This time around it's middle child and strong-willed Sloane, who has had more than her share of bad relationship experiences. So it's understandable when she's suspicious of her instant attraction to steer wrestler Jason Till.

She's not the only one surprised by the instant attraction, one that doesn't go away even when hundreds of miles separate them. Jason's number-one goal is to win the National Finals in his event. At least that was his main goal until Sloane Hartley walked into his life.

To reach their happily-ever-after, they have to make some important decisions about what they really want from life. And it's looking like the answer is each other.

Happy reading,

Trish

HER TEXAS RODEO COWBOY

———

TRISH MILBURN

HARLEQUIN® WESTERN ROMANCE

Recycling programs for this product may not exist in your area.

ISBN-13: 978-0-373-75773-2

Her Texas Rodeo Cowboy

Copyright © 2017 by Trish Milburn

Printed in U.S.A.

Trish Milburn writes contemporary romance for the Harlequin Western Romance line. She's a two-time Golden Heart® Award winner, a fan of walks in the woods and road trips, and a big geek girl, including being a dedicated Whovian and Browncoat. And from her earliest memories, she's been a fan of Westerns, be they historical or contemporary. There's nothing quite like a cowboy hero.

Visit the Author Profile page at Harlequin.com for more titles.

Chapter One

Jason Till applied the brakes on his truck at the cross-walk, allowing a group of older women holding bakery bags to cross the street. His stomach grumbled at the thought of fresh baked goods. He could almost taste the sugar. He'd not eaten since the fast-food breakfast sandwich early that morning in some small town off I-35. If he had a dollar for every time he'd grabbed a quick meal in such a place, he'd be stinking rich.

One of the women crossing the street smiled and gave him a big, friendly wave. He chuckled a little and waved back. Then he took his foot off the brake and slowly rolled on down Main Street, glancing briefly at the Welcome, Cowboys and Cowgirls sign that hung above the street, advertising the rodeo that would start in just a few hours.

He'd been to more small towns across the country than he could count, some of which had definitely seen better days. But Blue Falls, Texas, seemed to have a booming downtown judging by the number of people he noticed going in and out of the various businesses and walking along the sidewalks. He spotted everything from clothing shops to a bookstore to an old-fashioned hardware store that reminded him of the one he'd gone

to as a little kid with his grandfather the few times he'd
visited his mom's parents in Alabama. And the bakery sat at the corner of a cross street, tempting him to
make a pit stop.

His stomach rumbled, more insistent this time, but
he drove on past in favor of getting to the fairgrounds
and signing in for the competition. He'd grab something
there. He had no doubt there would be at least one concession stand where he could pick up a burger or some
barbecue. If he did well this weekend, he'd treat himself to the biggest cinnamon roll the Mehlerhaus Bakery had. He'd bet good money they had one damn near
the size of a hubcap. This was Texas, after all.

As he pulled into the fairgrounds, he was surprised
to see how many people were there already. Next to
the area filled with pickups, RVs and horse trailers was
a field covered with lines of open tents. Not the kind
that people camped in but rather ones used for festival
booths. Looked as if the people of Blue Falls were going
all out for rodeo weekend.

From what he'd heard from other riders, Blue Falls
had regular rodeos with a lot of the proceeds going to
local charities and community improvement projects.
But this weekend's event was the first time organizers
had offered a purse sizable enough to really attract extra
notice from those trying to up their standings and move
another step closer to competing at the Finals in Vegas
in December. Which was his ultimate goal. After years
of clawing his way to this point, he finally had a second
shot at the Finals. He'd made it three years ago, barely,
but had ended up in next-to-last place. This year might
be his last viable chance, so he had to make the most
of it. Choose the most advantageous rodeos to compete

in, ride in each one as if it were the Finals and not let anything get in his way.

And a nice payday was always pretty darn attractive. After all, if he was going to spend his career staring at highways, the dirt of arena floors and the backsides of steers, he'd like to be paid well for it.

He found a spot next to the pickup Bo Whittaker had been driving since Jason wrestled his first steer on the pro circuit. Bo was a bareback rider who had a good five years on Jason's own thirty, and he showed zero signs of retiring anytime soon. Bo was one of those guys Jason couldn't imagine doing anything other than rodeo, much like his own family. Hanging out with Bo was a bit like being with his dad, who'd also been a bareback rider before he'd had to retire from competition due to injury. Except the age difference, of course, and the fact that Jason's parents had been married since they were nineteen and Bo was a confirmed bachelor. Not that Bo didn't like the ladies, because that also wasn't in doubt.

Jason ran into the man himself as he was leaving the sign-in area. Bo held up a paper-wrapped sandwich half the size of his head.

"You gotta try one of these barbecue sandwiches," Bo said. "I'd sell my own grandma for one of these."

Jason laughed. "I have a feeling your grandma would have something to say about that."

Bo nodded. "She'd probably whack me upside the head with her cane."

Jason had met Bo's grandma and could totally see that happening.

He took his friend's advice and plunked down some cash for a huge pulled pork barbecue sandwich and a freshly squeezed lemonade. He took a bite while waiting for his change. His taste buds woke up from hibernation and sang a hymn glorifying the sandwich.

"Good stuff," he said to the woman who returned with his change. "Used to beef in Texas, but this hits the spot."

"My daddy was from West Tennessee and made a mean pork barbecue. I do my part to convert all these beef folk," she said.

Jason smiled. "Good luck with that."

He was pretty sure the state animal of Texas was a longhorn, and that wasn't just because they loved football.

Trying not to gobble down his sandwich like some sort of ravenous beast, he wandered toward the arena. A few people were already seated in the grandstands—diehards who'd arrived early to pick their favorite spots.

He took another swig of his lemonade as he eyed the arena. Pretty typical for an outdoor facility in a small town—dirt that had been worked loose on top of the hardpan beneath, ad banners affixed along the perimeter fencing, stock pens behind the chutes, large arena lights that would attract thousands of bugs once night fell.

His gaze halted when he spotted a woman leading a group of eight kids from the barn area toward the stock pens. He could tell she was talking to them as she pointed toward the still-empty pens. Was she a teacher and this some sort of school trip?

When the woman turned toward the arena, he got a better look at her. Though her face was partly shaded by her light-colored cowgirl hat, he could tell she was pretty. A blond braid descended to just below her shoulders. Her jeans appeared to fit her long legs to nice effect.

He spotted Bo back toward the barns, and something about the idea of him approaching this woman and the trailing youngsters had Jason tossing his now-empty cup and sandwich wrapper into the trash barrel and heading toward them.

"See that area there?" she said to the kids as Jason drew close enough to hear her. "That's where the cowboys wait their turn to ride in their events."

"Are they scared?" one little boy asked.

"Maybe sometimes," the woman said.

"Nah, we're too crazy to be scared," Jason said as he rested one arm along the top of the metal fencing that made up the stock pens.

The woman turned toward him, tipping back the front brim of her hat a bit. He had the urge to laugh at the way her eyebrows bunched together, but some sense of self-preservation told him that was a bad idea.

"Sorry to interrupt," he said. "Saw you all over here and thought I'd say hello and ask if I can help you out."

Her expression eased slightly. "We're just doing a tour of the facilities before the rodeo gets under way."

"Are you a rodeo cowboy?" a little girl he'd guess was maybe eight or nine years old asked.

"I am." He extended his hand to the girl. "I'm Jason. What's your name?"

The girl stared at his hand then up at the woman. When the blonde placed her palm against the child's back and nodded once, the girl extended her tiny hand and shook his.

"Phoebe."

Thinking maybe he looked intimidating to some-

one so much shorter than he was and being a stranger
to boot, he was careful not to hold her hand too firmly.

"That's a pretty name. Do you like rodeos?"

"We've never been to one," another boy, this one a
bit older, said.

Instead of asking more questions, Jason shifted his
attention to the woman and noticed she was watching
him as if sizing him up, determining if he was a threat
to her young charges. He got the feeling she wouldn't
hesitate to do whatever was necessary to protect them.

"Do you have any questions?" he asked the boy without taking his eyes away from his protector.

"Sloane said there are different events. What do you
do?"

Sloane. That must be the mystery blonde's name. It
fit her somehow, pretty but strong and no-nonsense.
He had no idea how he was able to garner that much
about her in only a handful of minutes, but his gut told
him he was right.

He smiled just a hint and shifted his gaze to the boy.
"I'm a steer wrestler."

"That's the one where you jump off the running
horse and tackle a cow with horns?"

Jason chuckled. "Something like that."

He figured a lesson on the differences between
steers, cows, heifers and bulls was probably a bit too
much detail for the youngsters.

The boy asked several more questions in quick suc-
cession, as if he were being tested to see how much
rodeo knowledge he could stuff into his brain in a certain amount of time. When he started to ask another,
Sloane held out her hand to halt him.

"That's enough, Daron. We've taken up enough of Jason's time," she said.

"It's okay," Jason said, drawing her attention back to him. "I don't mind."

Especially if it kept Sloane around a little longer.

A second woman joined the group, accompanied by another little girl. These two, however, he could tell were related. The woman made eye contact with him for a moment, offered a smile, but then shot Sloane a questioning look.

Sloane motioned toward the new arrivals. "My sister, Angel, and niece, Julia."

They didn't look as if they were blood-related, not with Sloane being blond and fair and Angel of Native American descent, but the country was full of blended families.

He extended his hand to Angel. "Jason Till. Nice to meet you."

Angel shook his hand. "You, too. Are you one of the riders?"

"Yes, ma'am."

"He's a steer wrestler," Daron said with so much enthusiasm that Jason couldn't help but smile.

"We should get to our seats," Sloane said.

"We've got plenty of time," Angel replied.

He caught the look of surprise Sloane shot her sister, and if he wasn't mistaken Angel reciprocated with one of mischief. Sloane, the surprised expression now totally gone as if it had never existed, turned to him.

"Thanks for taking the time to talk to the kids."

"No problem."

"Good luck tonight."

"Thank you. I'll do my best to put on a good show for these guys," he said as he motioned toward the kids.

She said nothing else, just offered a quick smile and nod before she turned all of her attention to directing the kids toward the grandstands. Little Phoebe looked over her shoulder at him and offered a shy wave. He waved back, surprised by the way her smile lifted his mood. It wasn't as if he was in a bad mood, but there was just something so sweet and pure about the little girl.

"I don't suppose you have any free time this weekend, do you?"

The question caught him totally off guard. Was Angel about to ask him out? Not that she wasn't pretty because she definitely was, but she wasn't the sister who had captured his attention.

Before he could answer, she motioned toward Sloane and the kids. "My sister runs camps for underprivileged kids, where they come out and spend a weekend on our ranch. They get exposure to the animals, camp outside, learn about ranch life. This is the first time we've brought them to a rodeo, and it seems as if they're interested in learning more. Thought maybe you could come out to the ranch and talk to them some more about what it's like to be a rodeo cowboy."

He'd never done anything like that before, but if he got to spend some more time with Sloane...well, it would sure beat hanging around the fairgrounds listening to tales of Bo's latest romantic exploits.

"I could do that."

"Great." She rifled through her purse, then pulled out a business card and handed it to him. "Just text me when's a good time for you and we'll make it work."

He gave her a nod and watched as she joined the

others. When he saw the curious look on Sloane's face, he bit his lip to keep from laughing. He knew that expression, having seen it from his own sister on more than one occasion. It promised payback like only a sibling could serve up.

When Sloane shifted her gaze to him, he tapped the brim of his hat with his index finger and offered what he hoped was a smile charming enough to relax her suspicion. When she merely turned away, he did laugh under his breath.

"I'm telling you, that one's going to be a tough nut to crack," Bo said as he joined Jason. "Lot easier ways to get some female company."

"Maybe some things are worth working for," he said as he gave Bo a backhanded slap to the chest, then headed toward the barn. He needed to get in the right headspace for the competition. After all, he had to put on a good show for the campers.

And if their camp counselor liked what she saw, all the better.

SLOANE HARTLEY STARED hard at her approaching sister. "You are up to something."

Angel made a *pffftt* sound as she reached Sloane. "I think you have me confused with our brothers. They're the ones always up to something."

Sloane propped her hands on her hips. "I've always heard it's the quiet ones you have to watch out for."

"I'm not that quiet."

"But you do fly under the radar."

"Not hard when my siblings have such big personalities."

"I feel as if I was just insulted."

Angel gently patted Sloane's cheek. "Not at all. I like your big personality. And Ben's approaching bearable now that he's a married man."

Sloane paused her interrogation long enough to get all the campers and Julia settled in the bleachers. As usual, Julia was striking up instant friendships with the other kids, something their mother had noticed and pointed out as proof that there needed to be more grandchildren running around the Rocking Horse Ranch. Well, Neil and Ben were both married now, so Sloane figured the ball was in their procreation court. She sure wasn't going to be a player in that game, at least not anytime soon. With her luck, never.

When she sank onto the bleacher seat next to her sister, she resisted glancing toward the barn to see if Jason the steer wrestler was still visible. Yes, the man was wicked good-looking, and she was afraid Angel had noticed Sloane's awareness of that fact.

"So, spill. What were you talking to him about?"

"Him?" Angel asked, all faux innocence.

"You know exactly who I'm talking about."

"You mean the handsome cowboy who couldn't take his eyes off you?"

"You sound like Mom."

Angel shrugged. "I call it like I see it."

"Whatever. Maybe you should ask him out."

"Nah. Not my type."

"What is your type?"

Angel leaned back against the empty bleacher behind them. "I don't know because I haven't met him."

Sure, Angel had a daughter, but that didn't mean Julia's father was the kind of guy Angel wanted to spend the rest of her life with. In fact, Sloane wasn't sure that normally mild-mannered Angel wouldn't coldcock Dave if she ever saw him again. If she didn't, there was a long line of Hartleys willing to do it for her.

"Listen," Angel said. "All I did was invite him out to the ranch to talk to the kids some more about rodeoing. I saw how interested they were in what he was saying."

"You did what? Are you crazy? We don't know the first thing about him. He could be a creep. Or have a rap sheet as long as my arm."

Angel turned partway toward Sloane. "Did it strike you that either of those things is true?"

"How would I know? I barely spoke to the man."

"Well, then, you can cure that when he's your camp's guest speaker."

Sloane started to protest again but was interrupted by her younger sister.

"You know I'd never do anything to put these kids, including my daughter, in danger. If it was just going to be us there, I wouldn't have invited him. But Dad and the guys will be close by. Not that I think the two of us couldn't take Jason down by ourselves."

"You got that right." If anyone posed a threat to these kids, who already had enough to worry about in their young lives, she'd take them out. A boot to the kneecap could bring down the biggest man.

Though her instinct told her Angel was right, that this Jason guy was fairly harmless. Except, perhaps, to her peace of mind. The moment she'd met his dove-gray gaze, she'd been thrown off-kilter. That wasn't a normal state of being for her. She'd come into contact with plenty of handsome men before, so what was it about Jason the steer wrestler that felt different?

Probably just that he'd seemed to pop up next to her

out of thin air. She'd not exactly been startled, rather caught off guard. Just when she'd reined in her initial increased-pulse reaction to his looks, however, he'd gone and been nice to the kids. It was as if he was trying to increase his tally of "I'm an awesome guy" points as fast as he could, before she could even figure out who he was.

No need to worry about it though. As long as he entertained the kids, she was cool with him talking to them. But it didn't matter how good-looking or charming he might be, she wasn't interested in a cowboy only in town for a weekend. They came and went. She didn't blame them. It was how they made their living or followed their passion. But if she ever ended up serious about a guy—and with her dating history, she wasn't even sure she wanted that—it wasn't going to be someone living that sort of nomadic lifestyle.

Her family had given her roots, and rodeo cowboys like Jason Till were about as rooted as a tumbleweed.

Chapter Two

From his seat in the saddle, Jason glanced toward the grandstands. He needed to concentrate on his ride, which was only moments away, but he couldn't keep himself from trying to catch a glimpse of Sloane.

The sound of laughter drew his attention back to the area around the chutes. Bo was sitting atop one of the gates and he hadn't missed where Jason had been looking.

"I thought you had some sense," Bo said.

Jason snorted. "And you're the authority on good sense?"

"Never claimed that."

Jason shifted his focus to the business at hand as he rode into the box, the steer was loaded into the roping chute and his hazer, Travis Morgan, got into position on the other side of the chute. Jason took a slow, deep breath, visualizing the next few seconds, something he'd done countless times before. He pictured tonight as another step closer to a national championship. Then he gave the chute man a quick nod of his head. The chute opened and the steer took off, shadowed by Travis. The moment the barrier rope around the steer's neck popped off, Jason gave chase. Maybe a couple of heartbeats passed as he leaned off the side of his horse, got his right arm in position on the steer and let his feet slide free of his stirrups. He dug his heels into the dirt, grabbed the left horn with one hand and the right horn in the crook of his other elbow. He pulled the steer off balance but the animal wasn't going to make it easy. Jason's boots furrowed the dirt as the steer tried to free itself. Finally, after what seemed like forever, he managed to throw the steer to the ground. Unfortunately, he ate a bit of dirt in the process.

He didn't even have to look to know it wasn't his best time ever. Cursing, he got to his feet and spit out the dirt as the steer trotted away down the arena. Despite the disappointing score, he took off his hat and waved to the cheering crowd. He wondered if Sloane and the kids were clapping, but he couldn't see them beyond the glare of the arena lights.

"Tough one," Travis said when they met up outside the arena.

"Yeah, wasn't my night." Even though he'd have bet money he was focused, had he actually still been distracted by thoughts of a certain blonde?

He considered seeking her out in the stands, but a hit of common sense kept his boots planted on the other side of the fence watching the rest of the bulldoggers. Bo was right. There were easier ways to enjoy some female company than seeking out someone who evidently wasn't all that interested in him. Someone who wouldn't distract him so much that he lost an opportunity to move up in the standings. Plus, he'd be gone from Blue Falls in a couple of days and on to New Mexico.

He tried not to think about the long drive and what life was like for normal people who had weekends and didn't have a longer relationship with the interstate system than they'd ever had with a woman. His parents were lucky they'd both been rodeo competitors. Neither ever had to leave the other behind when they hit the road. But that had never worked for Jason. He'd dated a couple of barrel racers and the daughter of a stock contractor, but none of those relationships had lasted more than a couple of months.

Why the devil was he thinking about relationships all of a sudden?

Maybe it had to do with his parents' upcoming anniversary and his sister's question—she wanted to know if he could take time to attend a party if she hosted one. Shannon had sounded so hopeful despite the fact that she probably hadn't intended to. Even though she had been the one to break with family tradition and not go into professional rodeo, she fully understood the importance of competing in as many events as possible, or at least enough with sizable prize money.

"You coming with us?" Travis asked as Jason removed the saddle from his horse. "Hear there's a good band playing at the local dance hall."

Jason shook his head. "Not tonight. Need some sleep."

"Don't tell me you're turning into an old fart."

"Just wait. You won't be young and able to operate on no sleep forever." In some professions, people were just getting started at thirty. But he'd been riding the circuit since he met the age requirement at eighteen.

Even though Travis was only seven years younger than Jason, sometimes that difference felt like three times what it was. He hadn't been lying about wanting to get some sleep, but the truth was he just wasn't in the mood to go drinking and dancing. Not when his mind refused to stop replaying his ride over and over, analyzing what he'd done wrong and how to make sure it didn't happen again.

But as he lay down in yet another generic motel room an hour later and stared at the ceiling, sleep didn't seem to be anywhere in the vicinity of Blue Falls. His thoughts abandoned his poor performance at the rodeo and drifted to Sloane... Was her last name Hartley like her sister's, or was that Angel's married name? Regardless of her surname, there was something that he couldn't put his finger on that kept bringing Sloane to the front of his mind. And he didn't think it was just because she was pretty.

Or maybe he was sleep deprived. For some reason he'd been sleeping like garbage lately. He'd been fixated so much on making this the year he got back to the Finals. Maybe he needed a brief break, a few hours to think about something else. Hopefully it would even help him ride better next time.

He rolled onto his side and turned on the bedside lamp. He picked up the business card Angel Hartley had given him and his phone. He'd take her up on her offer to go speak to the kids about rodeo, see if her sister's attitude toward him was any warmer in the light of day. If nothing else, it would beat hanging around the fairgrounds all day dwelling on his mistakes.

Before he could talk himself out of it, he sent Angel a text. He was surprised by how quickly she replied, confirming that ten the next morning was perfect.

As he turned the light back off, he smiled. It was nice to have something to look forward to, something that wasn't accompanied by the pressure to win.

"CAN WE RIDE real horses?" Daron asked as Sloane helped a little girl named Alice out of the saddle sitting atop a saddle rack in the barn's alley.

"You'll get to ride around the paddock with us helping you." The thing she always feared the most was one of the kids getting hurt, and she took every precaution against that happening.

She held Alice's little hand until she made her way to the ground via the hay bale steps.

"So, who wants to learn how to play horseshoes?"

"We actually have something else planned right now," Angel said.

Sloane gave her sister a questioning look for a moment before she realized what she must mean.

"Is that right?"

The sound of an approaching truck engine caused a long-suffering sigh to escape Sloane. She got enough teasing from her brothers and not-so-subtle hints from her mother about finding a good man. She didn't need it from her sister, too.

"I believe that's our special guest now," Angel said with way too much glee in her voice before heading out the door of the barn.

By the time Sloane gathered up the kids and ushered them outside, Jason was already out of his truck and talking to Angel. He held one of the recognizable bags from Mehlerhaus Bakery. When he spotted her, he lifted it as if she hadn't been able to see it before.

"I brought breakfast," he said.

Behind him, she saw the front door to the house open and out stepped her brothers. Normally, that protectiveness she saw in their stances would annoy the living daylights out of her, but this time it might actually prove amusing. She barely suppressed a smile.

"We ate hours ago. Some of us don't sleep half the morning," she said.

He'd probably been partying at the Blue Falls Music Hall until late. On rodeo nights, the place was filled to bursting with cowboys looking for a cold beer, a few spins around the dance floor and maybe a night with a pretty woman.

She couldn't knock the place. She enjoyed an evening out dancing and hanging with friends as much as the next person. But for some reason the thought of Jason picking up a woman and spending the night with her, then a few hours later strolling onto her ranch to speak to these innocent kids rubbed her the wrong way.

He lowered the bag and shrugged. "It's never too late for pastries."

Angel grinned at Sloane. "I have to agree with him there."

"Aren't you two going to introduce us?" her oldest brother, Neil, asked as he descended the steps, followed by Ben and Adam.

"That's Jason," Daron piped up. "He's a steer wrestler."

"Is he, now?" Neil eyed Jason like he did every man who came within close proximity of either of his sisters.

Jason extended his hand for a shake. "Jason Till. Your sisters invited me out to talk to the kids about the rodeo."

"Sister, singular," Sloane said under her breath, drawing a curious look from Daron and a couple of the other kids.

Neil took Jason's hand, and even from where she

stood she could tell big bro had made sure Jason knew just how strong he was. A glance at Ben and Adam showed they were doing a pitiful job of hiding their amusement.

She rolled her eyes. Okay, the scene ceased being funny and strode right into annoying. She wasn't a damsel in distress and she didn't need her brothers' protection. She didn't have any statistics to back it up, but she sincerely doubted guys who posed a threat showed up with a bag of fresh pastries.

"All right," she said. "Pastries for everyone."

The kids squealed and jumped up and down, making her smile and ending the testosterone-off.

She motioned everyone to the campsite in a shady area beyond the barn. The circle of tents surrounded log benches and a fire pit. Flying from a small flagpole was a blue flag with white lettering that said Camp Rocking Horse and sported the outline of the ranch's brand. The kids seated themselves on the logs, and Jason squatted in the center of the circle. She refused to notice how snug his jeans fit his backside in that position.

Yeah, right. She'd have to be dead for that to escape her notice.

"Okay, who likes cherries?" Jason asked.

Phoebe's hand and that of another girl named Ginny shot into the air.

"Good thing I got two, huh?"

He handed those out, followed by a variety of other Danish and doughnuts. When only one child remained empty-handed, he shifted his attention to Brent, the quietest of the bunch. His story hurt Sloane's heart, and she'd had to fight the urge to simply wrap the little boy in her arms and tell him everything would be okay. Of course, she couldn't know that. She got these kids for a weekend, to give them a little light and fun in their lives, a different environment. But then they had to go back to their group homes or to families that had problems of one sort or another. She'd never counted on seeing them leave being so difficult.

"What do you like, little man?"

Brent shrugged.

"Can I tell you a secret?"

"Okay," Brent said in the small voice she'd only heard a few times.

Jason leaned in toward Brent a little. "The best one is still in here. It's my favorite. Want to see what it is?"

Brent glanced toward her, and she gave him an encouraging smile. The boy returned his gaze to Jason and nodded.

Jason pulled a pastry from the bag and placed it on a napkin in his palm. "Behold, the cruller."

He said it with such awe and reverence that one would think he was displaying Excalibur rather than a piece of fried dough.

Angel leaned in next to her and whispered. "He's good with them."

Sloane couldn't disagree, but even that annoyed her for some reason.

After handing the cruller to Brent, Jason turned toward where Angel and Sloane stood.

"What about you ladies?" He glanced down into the bag. "I've still got glazed doughnuts and a couple of apple Danish."

"Doughnut, please," Angel said.

He gave the doughnut to Angel, then shifted his questioning gaze to Sloane.

"I'm good."

Beside her, Angel made a frustrated sound. "She'll take a Danish."

When Jason extended the pastry toward her, she almost kept her arms crossed. But she realized she was being unnecessarily prickly and accepted his offering.

"Thanks." When he placed the bakery bag down on an empty log bench, she pointed at it. "Aren't you having something? It's only fair since you've foisted a ton of sugar and calories off on the rest of us."

He patted his stomach. "Oh, trust me. I had plenty on the way out here."

Could have fooled her. Though he was wearing a button-down shirt that wasn't formfitting, she'd bet good money there was a nice set of solid abs lurking beneath the cloth.

Irritated at the direction of her thoughts, she took a giant bite of her Danish.

Jason sank onto the bench. "So, who has questions about being a rodeo cowboy?"

"How long have you been a cowboy?" Alice asked.

"For as long as I can remember. I started mutton busting when I was four years old."

"What's mutton busting?" Daron asked.

"It's where you ride a big woolly sheep. You wrap your legs around the sheep's body," Jason explained, making a circle with his arms, "and hang on to the wool with your hands and see how long you can ride without falling off."

"That sounds like fun," Brent said, surprising Sloane so much she was sure her eyes widened. It was the first time Brent had said anything without being asked a direct question.

"It was. It's how kids get interested in the rodeo."

"Are we going to do mutton busting?" a boy named Enrique asked. There was such a light in his dark eyes and excitement in his question that Sloane hated to burst his bubble.

"Sorry, but no."

"Why not?"

She glanced at Jason to find him watching her, also waiting for the answer to Enrique's question.

"We don't have sheep, for one." Not to mention the safety equipment and the level of liability insurance that such an event would require. Or the money for any of those things.

The looks and sounds of disappointment rekindled her irritation, not at the kids but at Jason for bringing up the topic in the first place.

Okay, so he was just answering a question, but still. What kid could resist the idea of riding a big, fluffy sheep? Heck, she would have totally done that as a kid if the opportunity had been there.

"I'm sure you're going to be doing a bunch of other fun stuff this weekend," Jason said.

Sloane gradually relaxed again as she watched the continued exchange between Jason and the kids. He never acted as if any of their questions were stupid, and he didn't talk down to them. It made her wonder if he had kids of his own. He didn't wear a wedding band, but that didn't mean anything. Some of the rodeo guys were probably like sailors with a girl in every port.

By the time her mom rang the bell signaling lunch was ready, Sloane had learned that Jason was from Idaho, he'd been competing as a professional since he was eighteen and he'd had six broken bones thanks to his career choice.

Angel herded the kids toward a couple of picnic tables next to the grilling station near the house.

"Are you eating with us?" Phoebe asked as she slipped her little hand into Jason's.

He smiled down at the girl. "I don't think they planned for the extra mouth to feed."

Sloane huffed at that. "You've never met my mother and her penchant for making twice as much food as needed."

"Please," Phoebe said.

"Well, how can I say no to such a nice invitation?"

Phoebe's lips stretched into a huge smile, and damn if Sloane didn't have to fight to keep from doing the same thing.

Phoebe shot off toward the picnic area as if she hadn't eaten both a hearty breakfast and a midmorning pastry.

Jason chuckled. "Sweet kids."

"Yeah. And resilient."

He gave her a questioning look.

"They all come from tough backgrounds. Some are from struggling, low-income homes. Several are in foster care for one reason or another. All of them have had to face more than they should at their age."

"That's sad."

"It is. They seem to like you though."

"And that annoys you."

"I didn't say that."

"You didn't have to." He grinned at her as he grabbed a ham-and-cheese sandwich and a couple of her mom's homemade oatmeal cookies.

"Sorry. I just don't know you, and these kids' safety is my responsibility."

"So this has nothing to do with the fact that your sister is trying to set us up?"

"Well, there goes my hope that it was obvious only to me."

"It's not a bad idea. I'm a decent guy."

"Perhaps you are, but you're also going to be long gone by tomorrow night." And her record of picking guys to date was far from stellar.

He nodded. "Fair enough."

Well, that reaction was unexpected. She'd thought he might try to encourage her to live a little, have some harmless fun. She wasn't a fuddy-duddy and wasn't on the hunt for a forever kind of guy, but she also wasn't hot on the idea of being with a guy who'd no doubt been with several women before her and would be with several afterward. She wasn't judging that choice. It just wasn't for her.

Of course, she often doubted a serious relationship was for her either. She'd seen at a young age what loving someone too much could do to a person. The one time she'd believed she might have a future with a guy, she'd been proven wrong in a way that still stung years later. The relationships since then had really ended before they started.

They walked toward one of the picnic tables. Though her father and Neil had ridden out partway through Jason's Q and A with the campers, Ben was still keeping an eye on things from outside his saddle shop. And it was a safe bet that Adam was lurking nearby, too.

"I'm guessing your brothers have scared off a number of dates for you and Angel over the years."

"They try, the annoying brats. But Angel and I can hold our own."

"That does not surprise me."

"You don't even know us."

"Call it gut instinct."

They sat in silence long enough for each of them to eat their sandwiches. She listened to Daron at the opposite end of the table talking to a couple other boys about how he could ride a sheep all day and not fall off. He was so animated that she had to hide a smile behind her hand. Beside her, Jason chuckled.

"That one is full of personality," Jason said.

"Yep."

"What's his story?"

"From a single-parent home, the youngest of six kids. They struggle to get by." And how heartbreaking was it that Daron's story was one of the happier ones?

She noticed Brent watching them silently from the other table. "I think someone is a fan."

He glanced in the direction she nodded. "Hey, Brent, can you help me out? I have more cookies than I can eat. You want one?"

Brent slid off his seat and came to stand at the end of their table. Jason handed him one of the cookies that Sloane had no doubt Jason could eat with no problem.

"Do you have to be big to ride in the rodeo?" Brent asked.

"Not all the time. One of the toughest bull riders I know isn't much bigger than you."

Brent's eyes widened.

"Okay, let's not put wild ideas in the child's head." She could just see one of these kids going home and telling their family or guardians that a cowboy encouraged them to ride a two-thousand-pound animal with three-foot horns.

She expected Jason to leave after lunch, but he hung around for a game of horseshoes. He gave pointers to the kids on throwing technique and engaged in some good-natured ribbing that had them giggling. Part of her wanted to be annoyed, but she was too thankful to see the kids' smiles and hear their laughter.

"You're good with them," she said when he came to stand next to her, echoing Angel's earlier observation.

"I've had practice with my sister's kids, six-year-old twins."

"Boys or girls?"

"One of each."

Well, that explained it. He was probably used to being the cool uncle, which was basically what he'd been today. All the fun stuff with none of the responsibility.

"I better get going," he said. "Thanks for inviting me out."

"You have Angel to thank for that."

"Well, then, thanks for not chasing me off with a pitchfork."

Phoebe ran up to them. "Are you leaving?"

Jason placed his hand gently atop Phoebe's light brown hair. "Yeah, this cowboy's got to go try to make some money."

"Can we go to the rodeo again tonight?" Phoebe asked, drawing a chorus of agreement from the other kids.

Angel smiled as she picked up the last of the horseshoes. Sloane was going to get her sister back for creating this monster and making Sloane the bad guy.

"Not tonight." At the groans of disappointment, she said, "We've got a hayride and a big cookout planned. My dad makes the best burgers in Texas."

"And there's a meteor shower," Angel said. "We can lie out on blankets and watch them streak across the sky."

Brent looked up at Jason, who must have seemed as tall as a skyscraper to the little guy. "Are you coming back tomorrow?"

Jason started to say something but stopped and looked at Sloane.

"I'm sure Jason has things to do." Like drive right out of Blue Falls and on to the next rodeo in the next town in an endless string that would stretch out for the rest of the year, only stopping when winter arrived.

"I have time, if you don't mind," Jason said.

She ignored a little flutter of excitement in the center of her chest. It was the height of stupidity, especially when all her attention needed to be on the kids this weekend. But then she saw the naked look of hope on Brent's face and she simply couldn't deny him another chance to be near his new hero—even if she thought there were way better heroes for a little boy to idolize.

"Feel free to come by," she said. "But we're going to have a lesson on mucking out stalls."

"I have lots of experience in that department." Jason grinned.

Damn if that grin probably hadn't charmed more than one woman out of her panties. If not for the camp this weekend, she wasn't 100 percent sure that she would be able to resist.

Chapter Three

Through an incredible streak of luck—a good draw for him and some poor performances from others—Jason ended up placing higher in the rodeo than he'd expected after his first night's performance. High enough that he gained a spot in the national standings. He was in such a good mood that after a hearty breakfast at the Primrose Café, he bought some flower bouquets on his way out to the Rocking Horse Ranch.

Sloane had been right, of course. He would be leaving town later today, so getting involved wasn't a wise decision. But it didn't keep him from thinking about her, or evidently wanting to buy her a bouquet of flowers. He'd been halfway back to his truck outside the florist shop when he wondered if she might not be a flowers kind of gal.

But all women liked flowers, right?

To be on the safe side and to keep himself from potentially looking like a fool, he went back in and bought more flowers. If he brought bouquets for every female in residence at the ranch, all bases were covered.

True to her word, Sloane was giving a lesson on mucking out stalls when he arrived. She paused for a split second when she saw him enter the barn. Was she surprised that he'd actually come back? He hoped it was a pleasant surprise.

The kids hadn't noticed him yet so he leaned against one of the stalls, the flowers hidden behind his back, as he listened to her tell the kids that having horses was a big responsibility. They had to be fed, watered, brushed, their health maintained and, yes, their poop scooped.

A chorus of "Eew!" made him chuckle to himself as she used the pitchfork to lift a section of soiled hay and deposit it in the wheelbarrow.

Little Phoebe was the first to notice him. When the wide grin appeared on her face, she called out, "Jason!" and ran toward him, his heart expanded the way it did whenever he got to visit Caleb and Lily.

He squatted in time for Phoebe to wrap her arms around his neck in a hug.

"You came back."

"I said I would."

She pulled away and stepped to his side. "Why are you hiding flowers behind your back?"

"As a surprise for you." He brought one of the smaller bouquets around to give to her.

Her smile would brighten the darkest day. He suddenly wondered what her story was and hoped it wasn't too bad. Anything that took away that smile would be a crime.

Phoebe brought the flowers up to her nose and sniffed them. "They're so pretty."

"Is it okay if I give the other girls some flowers, too?"

Phoebe nodded. "They smell nicer than the horse poop."

He barked out a laugh, especially when he caught Sloane rolling her eyes. "I agree with you there."

Jason walked over to Alice and the other girls in the group, including Angel's daughter, Julia, then handed them all miniature bouquets identical to Phoebe's.

"Did you bring some for Angel and Sloane?" Alice asked.

"I did." He extended a bouquet to Angel, who stood on the opposite side of the alley from Sloane and her pitchfork.

"Thanks." She sniffed them. "Phoebe is right. They do smell better than horse poop."

The word *poop* got all the kids to giggling again.

"Do you like my mom?" Julia asked as she eyed him.

"She's very nice," he said, gathering from the child's question that perhaps Angel was single. He'd heard nothing about a husband or boyfriend the day before.

"Do you want to take her on a date? Boys bring girls flowers when they want to go out on dates."

"Julia," Angel said, gently scolding. She shifted her gaze across to her sister. "Jason doesn't want to go on a date with Mommy."

Sloane pointed accusingly at Angel with the hand holding the pitchfork.

He extended one of the last two bouquets toward Sloane. "Your aunt, however, is a different story."

He couldn't tell for sure because of the hat she wore and the fact that she was no doubt warm from cleaning the stall, but he thought color rose in Sloane's fair cheeks. She seemed at a loss for how to respond, and he considered he'd made a mistake saying what he had. He'd put her on the spot, and after she'd made it clear the day before she wasn't interested in someone who'd be leaving town even before the campers would.

But he didn't have to leave yet. He could stick around

a couple more days and still make it to the next rodeo in plenty of time. Considering what she'd said the day before, he should leave now. But he flat-out didn't want to. He wanted to get to know Sloane Hartley better. Despite her eye rolls and distancing behavior, he suspected there was a lot more to her. Like why she held these camps for kids who came from difficult backgrounds.

Common sense tried to convince him he was making a mistake. After all, being distracted by her was most likely the cause of his poor ride two nights earlier. Until this year was over, he should steer clear of distractions—even really pretty ones.

Especially really pretty ones.

"Those are lovely," said a voice from behind them.

He continued looking at Sloane a moment longer, but she didn't make a move to take the bouquet he offered. Shot down, he turned to face her mom.

"I'm glad you think so because these are for you," he said, lifting the final bouquet.

"Well, that was sweet of you," Mrs. Hartley said as she stepped closer and accepted the flowers. "These will look great in my kitchen." She slipped her arm through his. "He's a good one. A smart woman would snatch him up while he's still available." She looked up at him. "You are available, aren't you?"

"Yes, ma'am."

Sloane didn't roll her eyes this time, but he imagined her thinking about doing exactly that. Instead, she turned back to the stall and continued her lesson.

Mrs. Hartley patted him on the arm. "Don't let her thorny exterior scare you off."

"It'll take more than that. I wrestle ornery steers for a living."

Mrs. Hartley smiled at that, patted his arm once again, then stepped away. "Let me take Sloane's flowers and put them in water. I'll be sure to put them someplace she can't miss them."

"Thank you, ma'am."

"No need for the formality. Call me Diane."

He nodded.

"And if you don't have to leave, make sure you stay for dinner."

"Thanks. I appreciate the invitation." During the rodeo season, home-cooked meals were few and far between. No cowboy with any sense turned one down.

He had a funny feeling Sloane might not feel the same about the invitation. That just meant he had his work cut out for him to change her mind.

SLOANE SHOULD HAVE known something like this was coming after Neil and Ben both got married. There'd been enough teasing around the dinner table that she was next despite her efforts to guide the conversation in any other direction. But she refused to be pushed into a situation not of her own choosing. She loved her family, but that didn't mean she'd let them have their way.

A part of her realized Jason was a bit of a pawn in the current situation, too, but he wasn't helping matters by bringing her flowers, being adorable with the kids and charming her mother. That trifecta would totally work with most women. She wasn't most women.

He came to stand next to the stall she'd just finished cleaning as Angel led the kids outside for another activity.

"How can I help?" he asked.

She exited the stall and closed the door, then pointed at the wheelbarrow beside him. "You can empty that."

Dang it, he didn't hesitate or question her. Instead, he grabbed the handles and headed out of the barn. He didn't even ask where the manure pile was. Chances were good he grew up on a ranch though, so it wasn't as if he was a city slicker with no clue what he was doing.

She waited until he was out of sight before she placed her hands on her hips, looked up into the rafters and took a deep breath. Just a little while longer and he would leave. He would take his long legs, infectious smile and nice-guy act right out of town on his way to the next rodeo.

But was it an act? She wasn't sure, which bothered her. He'd said he wanted to go out with her, which gave him a motive to be nice. But damn if the pastries, the flowers and his kindness didn't have a ring of truth.

But so had Blake's words of love once upon a time, a claim that hadn't been enough to keep him in Blue Falls and with her.

She blew out a breath and headed outside, where Angel had the kids lined up along the fence, telling them about the cattle on the opposite side. Before they'd ridden out to deliver scours vaccines to the pregnant cows, her dad and brothers had herded a dozen head of cattle into an area where the kids could see them while remaining safe.

"Does anyone know what kind of cattle these are?" Angel asked.

"Longhorns," Daron called out.

"That's right. Some of these guys can weigh up to or even more than two-thousand pounds."

"Whoa!" Daron said, and was echoed by several other kids.

After Angel ended her lesson about the cattle, they had the kids wash their hands and then head to the picnic area again for the final meal of the camp. Just the riding lessons remained before the kids would be picked up and taken home.

Sloane watched as the kids went through the line to get their food—chicken tenders, potato salad and brownies today. Though she tried to keep her attention off Jason, it was way more difficult than she'd have liked. When he seated himself next to Brent, a suspicious flutter in her chest made her worry that her mom's and Angel's attempted matchmaking was getting to her.

No, she couldn't let that happen. She was stronger than that.

And yet, when she got her food, she made her way to the spot opposite Jason and Brent. Okay, so curiosity about their topic of conversation got the better of her.

Jason didn't even look up at her when she sat down. Instead, he kept his entire focus on the little boy beside him.

"Do you think I could be a rodeo cowboy?" Brent asked.

"I think you can be whatever you want as long as you're willing to work hard for it. Can you do that?"

Brent nodded with more enthusiasm than she would have ever imagined he possessed. Somehow, Jason had encouraged the shy little boy to break out of his shell.

"I want to be a steer wrestler just like you."

While Brent seemed excited, witnessing the exchange broke Sloane's heart. He'd obviously formed a quick but strong attachment to Jason. She worried that

Brent didn't comprehend that after today he'd probably never see Jason again. And it might be years before Brent even got a chance to attend another rodeo, let alone have an opportunity to practice a skill like steer wrestling. She had a hard time picturing him ever being big enough to tackle such a dangerous profession. Her hope was that he was young enough that he'd probably go through at least another dozen answers to the question of what he wanted to be when he grew up. Memories of this camp, of Jason the steer wrestler, would fade.

She wondered if her own memories of Jason would fade, as well. When was the last time she'd had such a difficult time keeping her gaze from wandering to a guy? She refused to believe it had been Blake more than a decade ago. But her two short-lived relationships since then hadn't involved any irresistible urges to watch someone's every move. She supposed that should have been a clue they were duds in the making.

"Then I have no doubt you can do it," Jason said and ruffled Brent's hair, earning a big grin from the boy.

Sloane couldn't help grinning, too. Of course that's when Jason finally looked at her. But she didn't hide her smile. He was so kind to the kids, especially Brent, who perhaps needed the attention the most.

When lunch was over, she could feel the excitement level of the kids rise by the moment. They were at the point of the weekend they'd been looking forward to— being able to ride an actual horse. Without being asked, Jason helped get the horse saddled and moved into the paddock. After some pointers and safety tips, Jason lifted little Alice into the saddle.

At first, Alice looked anxious and held on to the saddle horn with a white-knuckle death grip.

"It's a long way up there, huh?" Jason asked.

Alice nodded.

"Don't worry. We won't let you fall." He nodded to where Sloane stood next to Alice, ready to grab the little girl if anything unexpected happened.

Alice relaxed enough so that by the time her turn was over, she was smiling.

"You're officially a cowgirl now," Jason said as he lifted her out of the saddle and handed her over the fence to Angel and Mom, who had joined the group after cleaning up following lunch.

Alice beamed so much that Sloane thought if Jason ever retired from rodeo, he might have a future working with kids.

For the next hour, one kid after another was given their time in the saddle. Little Brent looked as if he'd died and gone to heaven. Daron whooped as if he'd conquered Everest, making everyone laugh. Last up was Phoebe. She'd shown the same excitement as the rest of the kids, until she got near the horse. She balked, no doubt at its size.

Jason crouched in front of her. "I bet you'll be the best cowgirl yet," he said so that none of the other girls could hear.

"I'm scared."

Jason nodded. "I understand. It's scary to be on an animal so much bigger than you. But Sloane and I are right here. We won't let anything happen to you."

Phoebe looked at the horse again, not totally willing to let go of her apprehension. "Okay."

It wasn't the most enthusiastic response, so Sloane took her time easing Phoebe into the saddle and settling her little feet in the stirrups. Then she gently squeezed the girl's jeans-clad leg and gave her an encouraging smile. "You're very brave."

Jason led the horse slowly around the same path all the other kids had taken. All was going well and she could see Phoebe gradually relaxing when all of a sudden the horse whinnied and sidestepped. She'd been around horses long enough to realize the animal was about to rear.

Phoebe cried out in alarm in the same moment and released her grip on the saddle horn. Sloane acted on pure adrenaline-fueled instinct and grabbed Phoebe, pulling her free of the saddle. She held the girl close and took several quick steps away from the horse just as Jason shot her a meaningful look and gripped the bridle to lead the horse in the opposite direction.

Sloane didn't have to hear the rattle to know what had spooked the horse. Her heart raced at the thought that Phoebe could have been thrown and injured, that the horse could have hurt any one of them in its fear of the rattlesnake, that Jason, leading the way, could have been bitten. But none of those things happened, and she had to focus on calming Phoebe.

"Shh," she said. "It's okay. The horse just got a little feisty. See, everything is fine now." She turned so that Phoebe, who was attached to her like cling wrap, could see Jason rubbing the horse's face to soothe him.

Jason noticed what she was doing and offered Phoebe a big smile and a wave. "You did great. All those barrel racers in the rodeo better watch out. You'll give them a run for their money."

Sloane wasn't sure Phoebe would ever get on a horse again, but it was good of Jason to try to reassure the girl and get her mind off her fear. Sloane felt as if she could use some soothing herself, but she couldn't allow her inner turmoil to show. Not with the kids all watching. She wanted them to go away from this weekend with a positive experience and something they could look back on with fondness.

Jason casually looked toward where the snake no doubt was, then gave a slight nod to her in the opposite direction. Unwilling to put Phoebe on the ground even if she thought the girl would go for it, she took a circular route back toward the area where the rest of the kids were sitting. As she drew close, she saw the hint of worry in her sister's and mom's eyes. They, too, were trying to hide it from the kids.

"Well, that was exciting," Sloane said where everyone could hear. "I think Phoebe and the rest of you make a fine bunch of cowboys and cowgirls. Don't you all agree?"

Claps and cheers filled the air, and Phoebe leaned back to look her in the eye. "Is the horse okay?"

Sloane pointed at Jason, who was leading the horse toward the back side of the barn. "Yep. I think he's just tired."

"Maybe he can take a nap now."

"Maybe he can." Sloane smiled, grateful the little girl's fear was beginning to subside.

If only she could slow her own racing pulse as easily.

"Well, I think it's time we all enjoy one more brownie," her mom said. "Anybody agree with me?"

As expected, the kids were in complete agreement and followed Diane toward the house. Phoebe gave Sloane a hug before wriggling down to the ground and joining the others. Angel appeared as if she was about to ask Sloane a question, but Sloane motioned for her to go with the group.

She took a couple of deep breaths before she headed toward the barn. When she stepped into the shady interior, she found Jason with a gardening hoe in hand. He was watching the line of kids file into the house, obviously wanting them safely out of sight before he went back into the field to dispatch the rattler.

"I can do that," she said. Though she normally shot the snakes, that wasn't the best option with all the campers within earshot.

"I got it." He looked at her. "I think you better sit down. You look like you're about to faint."

"That happens when a kid in my care almost takes a tumble out of the saddle." She pressed her palm against the sudden sick feeling in her stomach.

She was barely aware of Jason moving before he pulled her close. "It's okay. Phoebe's fine. The horse is fine. The only one not going to be fine is that snake."

Some part of Sloane's brain was screaming, *Danger! Abort!* And the danger had nothing to do with the snake. Maybe the common sense telling her to pull away from Jason would engage later, but right now she gave it a boot to the backside and let him comfort her.

And tried really hard not to think about just how good it felt to be held in those strong, muscular arms.

Chapter Four

Sloane sure didn't feel thorny as Jason held her in his arms. In fact, while he could tell she was fit and strong, there was still a feminine softness to her, a sweet scent despite the fact that she'd been out in the sun and around the barn and horses. Unfortunately, he was only able to enjoy the feel and smell of her for a few moments before she pulled away and stepped free of his touch.

Probably for the best.

A quick glance at her face didn't show embarrassment or even anger. Rather, she acted as if they'd done nothing more than say a passing hello to each other.

"Thanks for taking care of the snake," she said without making eye contact, reminding him of what he'd been about to do.

Jason turned and headed toward the rear exit of the barn.

"Jason."

He stopped and glanced back at her.

"Just, uh… Thanks again."

She didn't elaborate, and he got the impression that maybe it might be difficult for her to even do so. Thinking he wouldn't mind holding her any time she needed it, he gave her a quick nod and headed out in search of the rattlesnake. He was usually a live-and-let-live kind of guy, but the thought of that snake striking one of the kids... Well, it wasn't going to happen if he could help it.

It took him a bit to find the rattler, but only a moment to dispatch him to the reptilian afterlife. He headed back to the barn, leaving the carcass for the buzzards.

When he reached the barn, Sloane was gone. That didn't surprise him. Though he hadn't known her long, he was still pretty certain she wasn't one to show weakness very often. She probably saw accepting a hug from him as a character flaw. As he replaced the hoe where he'd found it, he wondered what made her so independent. While her sister seemed every bit as able to handle herself, there was an extra wall around Sloane.

As he exited the barn, he eyed his truck and considered leaving. Chances were if he took Mrs. Hartley up on her offer of dinner, things would just be awkward with Sloane after the impromptu hug in the barn. But he hadn't been able to help himself. He'd understood why she'd been upset. Having one of her campers injured or bitten by a poisonous snake would have been really bad for a number of reasons, including the fact that it might have spelled the end for her camps. And it didn't take Einstein to figure out they meant a lot to her. Why, he didn't know, but the why didn't really matter. It was a good thing she was doing, and he hoped she would be able to continue doing it.

The sound of horses approaching drew his attention to the right. Sloane's dad and brothers rode into view and headed toward the barn. The oldest, Neil, saw him first, then scanned the rest of the area. As he came close, Neil's gaze fixed on Jason.

"The kids are gone already?"

"No, they're in the house. Your mom distracted them with a promise of more brownies."

"Distracted them from what?" Ben, the second brother asked, a note of what could be interpreted as accusation in his voice.

Jason didn't take offense. After all, he was plenty protective of Shannon, even if she was a couple years older than him. He gestured with his thumb back over his shoulder toward the paddock.

"Had a rattler make a visit, scared the horse we were using with the kids. But everyone is fine and the snake is no longer a problem."

The looks of concern on their faces eased.

"Diane tells me you're staying for dinner," Mr. Hartley said.

Mrs. Hartley must have called or texted her husband.

"She did invite me, sir. Thinking maybe I ought to head out though."

"Oh, no. If you don't stay now, she'll think one of us ran you off and we'll never hear the end of it." A spark of humor lit the man's eyes as he took off his hat and wiped the sweat from his forehead.

Jason glanced at the other Hartley men and sensed not exactly an acceptance but an easing of potential hostility.

Ben shrugged. "He's not wrong. Plus, Mom is a great cook."

"I could tell that already."

"That was nothing." Adam laughed a little as he gave what seemed like a meaningful look to his brothers. "She really goes all out when she's trying to impress company."

"She doesn't have to go to the trouble. My meals usually come from a drive-through window."

"Don't let her hear you say that," Mr. Hartley said. "She'll want to adopt you like she did this bunch."

The slight nod toward his sons explained the obvious difference in heritage between Sloane and Angel. So all the Hartley siblings were adopted? Of course, it didn't matter if they weren't blood-related. Adopted siblings teased each other the same way he and Shannon did, the way Caleb and Lily were already doing even at their young age.

"Well, my mom might have something to say about that," Jason said. "She's kind of partial to me."

At that moment, a van rolled up the driveway. As the driver parked next to Jason's truck, the front door of the house opened and out came Sloane with the kids. The van must be their ride back to their homes. He wondered what they were going back to. He knew Daron's situation but not those of the others. He glanced at sweet little Phoebe, Alice, all the other kids. Especially Brent, who even at this distance he could tell was already withdrawing again. Jason suddenly wanted to shield the kids from whatever hardships waited for them. He'd been lucky growing up, but he knew plenty of guys on the circuit who hadn't been. He'd seen the results, too. The drinking, the divorces, the broken families.

Sure, there were also plenty of people who grew up in hard situations who overcame it and made something good of their lives. He just hoped these kids followed that path.

Phoebe broke away from the group, holding her little bouquet of flowers in a jar of water. When she got close, he saw how shiny her eyes were, filled with un-shed tears.

"I wanted to say goodbye," she said, looking up at him.

Jason sank to one knee. "I'm glad I got to meet you."

Phoebe wrapped her arms around him, splashing a little water on his shirt. But he didn't care about that. She could pour the whole jar down his back.

"I don't want to leave," she said, sniffling a little.

He wanted to reassure her, to tell her everything would be okay. But how could he do that when he didn't even know what she was going back to?

"Hey, you became a cowgirl this weekend. Cowgirls are strong and can do whatever they set their minds to." When she stepped back, he pointed toward Sloane and Angel. "You can grow up to be like them. Or maybe a barrel racer."

"Then I could see you at rodeos."

He couldn't bring himself to tell her he'd be long re-tired before she was old enough to compete. "Maybe."

Something made him hesitate while he was escorting her back to where the rest of the kids stood talking to Sloane, Angel, Julia and the van driver, a middle-aged woman he'd guess was some sort of caseworker. On impulse, he reached up and brought the leather thong necklace he wore over his head.

"You see this?" he said, indicating the little carved wooden horseshoe hanging from the leather. "It's for good luck. I want you to have it."

Her eyes widened as he put the necklace over her head. She lifted the little horseshoe to look at it. "Thank you." And then she kissed him on the cheek and his heart melted.

"You're welcome." A glance at Sloane told him that it was time for Phoebe to go. He stood and offered her his hand. She put her much-smaller one in his and walked beside him back toward the others.

After saying several goodbyes to the kids, he noticed Brent hanging back and not speaking or making eye contact. It gave Jason a bad feeling in his stomach, a knot of concern wrapped in a layer of nausea.

"You okay, little man?" he asked Brent.

All the boy did was shrug. Jason experienced the strong urge to pick up the boy and keep him. Not only was that thought shocking but also totally unfeasible. Instead, he lowered himself to Brent's level so he could make eye contact.

"You really impressed me this weekend. Remember all you learned here. I know you're going to grow up and do great things. Don't ever let anyone tell you different, okay?"

It was a weak one, but Brent did manage a nod. He looked toward the van then back at Jason. "I'm never going to see you again, am I?"

Jason felt as if he'd been sucker punched in the heart. How did Sloane go through this over and over?

"Never say never. Life has a funny way about it." He wished he could tell the boy something more hopeful, more definite, but he wasn't willing to outright lie to him.

As the kids climbed into the van and Angel helped the driver get everyone buckled in, Sloane came to stand next to him.

"This is the worst part of what you do, isn't it?"

"Yeah," she said. "I can't fix everything though. I

had to come to grips with the fact that I can only do this small part, give them some good memories."

He got the impression she wasn't as okay with not being able to do more as she claimed.

Part of him didn't want to know, but a stronger part made him ask, "Phoebe and Brent, what are their stories?"

Next to him, Sloane sighed. "Both in foster care. Phoebe's parents died in a car crash when she was two, and there weren't any members of her family willing to take her. Brent..." Sloane paused, and Jason would swear he could hear the lump in her throat. "His mother was a drug addict. She overdosed and died in their house when he was four. By the time the police found him, he'd been in the house with his mom for three days."

Jason cursed. The boy's words about never seeing Jason again took on a new, horrible significance. No wonder the kid was quiet and withdrawn. How much did he remember about what he'd gone through? Did it haunt him?

"How do you do this, sending them back?"

"No choice. All I can do is give them a break from their lives."

He shifted his gaze from the van to Sloane. "You do more than that. You show them that a different life is possible."

Sloane looked shocked at his words. He was equally surprised she hadn't come to that conclusion herself.

"You're pretty damn amazing, Sloane Hartley."

JASON'S COMPLIMENT STUNNED Sloane so much that she found herself at a loss for how to respond. "Um...nothing really amazing about trying to help out where I can."

"I disagree. The world is full of people who don't care enough to do something like this."

Part of her knew he was right, but she'd also crossed paths with plenty of people who were giving, too. She didn't have to look any further than her adoptive parents.

Thankfully, the van making its departure drew Jason's attention away. The combination of his words of praise and the way he'd been looking at her, as if she was some sort of saint, made her uncomfortable.

The kids had their faces pressed up against the windows, waving at them. Sloane made herself smile and wave back, maintaining the positivity for them right up to the last moment they could see her. Jason was right about one thing. It was damned hard to send the kids back after getting to know them, especially if she thought about what many of them would face when they returned home.

Best not to dwell on it, however. It wouldn't make any difference in their lives and only serve to invite depression into her own. She'd been down that road and she never wanted to travel it again.

"Well, where you headed next?" she asked.

"According to your mom, dinner with your family."

Of course her mom had invited him to dinner. That didn't mean he had to accept.

"Don't feel obligated. She's always inviting people to dinner. She has this compulsive need to feed people."

"I thought about leaving, but I was informed by your dad and brothers that if I bailed they would never hear the end of it."

Inside her head, she growled. If everyone in her family was joining forces to set her up, she was going to have a sudden need to be elsewhere. She glanced toward the house and took a calming breath. The best way to handle the situation was probably to act as if she didn't care. Maybe she could even convince herself of that.

"Well, you're in for a treat. My mom is the best cook in Texas."

"Lucky me."

She didn't look at Jason as she turned to go inside, unwilling to seek out the answer to whether his response was about more than his taste buds' good fortune. As he followed her across the threshold of the front door, she headed for the kitchen, leaving Jason to navigate his own way through the sea of Hartleys.

Her mom looked up at her entry. "Where's Jason?"

Sloane pretended she didn't notice the unspoken question about whether Jason had already left. Instead, she made a vague gesture over her shoulder. "In the living room."

Normally, she'd have some faith in the male members of her family to run off any potential suitors. But from what Jason had said, it sounded as if they were on board with her mom's matchmaking efforts. And there was no mistaking that her inviting Jason to dinner was exactly that.

"Oh, good. He's such a nice guy, so good with the kids."

Play it cool. "Yeah, this was a good group. Easy to interact with them." All of which was true, but she hoped it also made the point that Jason wasn't anything special.

Except what if he was? She'd been envious of how easily he'd fit in with the kids, how quickly they'd come to adore him. She told herself that was a good thing, that the point was for the kids to have a good time. So what if she was the one who'd started the camps? The person who did most of the legwork? That she'd dreamed of making the camps a reality for years before she'd been able to launch them and still had hopes of expanding and helping even more kids?

She roped her runaway thoughts, remembering that she needed to be realistic. Someday she'd reach her lofty goals, but it was necessarily going to be a slow build because of the time, manpower and, most of all, money available. She wasn't the most patient of people, so it was hard to think about how long it was going to take her to reach her goals. But she had to be thankful she was able to do anything at this point, especially with the financial hits the ranch had taken in the past year. She already struggled with the guilt of being a drain on the collective resources when her siblings were working on ways to bring in more streams of revenue.

"You okay?" her mom asked, making Sloane realize she'd gotten lost in her tangle of thoughts.

"Yeah, just thinking about ways to improve the camps."

"Maybe convince Jason to help out with each of them. The kids seemed to love him."

Sloane engaged her best pivot by saying, "I saw an article about an elephant sanctuary that sells paintings done by the elephants. It's not so much that it's good art but rather a way people can connect and get something unique while supporting a good cause. Maybe we could sell hoof paintings by the cows and horses, have them step in paint and then walk over the paper."

"That might work."

The response didn't come from her mother but rather

Jason, who'd managed to enter the room without Sloane noticing.

Remember, act casual.

Sloane lifted an eyebrow. "Don't tell me you're an art expert in addition to steer wrestler and kid whisperer."

Ugh, did that make it sound as if she admired him too much? She didn't dare make eye contact with her mom to find out.

"No, but my sister works in marketing for a non-profit in Boise."

Of course she did. Again, Sloane mentally told herself to chill and look on the bright side. Maybe the world had put Jason in her path not as some sort of cosmic romantic setup but so that she might garner some helpful hints for how to move another step closer to being able to offer ranch experiences to hundreds of kids.

"If she has some ideas to toss my way, I'd be grateful."

"That was nice of you to offer, Jason," her mom said as she placed a platter of barbecue ribs on the table, then patted him on the upper arm.

"Least I could do considering I might just eat half those ribs."

Her mom laughed. "Good thing we have plenty more where those came from."

When her mom turned back toward the kitchen, Jason caught Sloane's gaze and gave her what appeared to be a teasing smile. Resisting the urge to snort and roll her eyes, she instead went to the cabinet that contained the glasses and started pulling out enough for everyone.

She hated the tense, fidgety feeling enveloping her as she did her best to go through the normal motions of preparing for a family meal. Something about Jason specifically knocked her off-kilter because this wasn't the first time her mom had tried to nudge her toward a guy. Though she wondered why her mom had zeroed in on a man who would be leaving town as soon as he got a good, home-cooked meal in his belly.

When Arden and Mandy, her sisters-in-law, showed up, indicating that Neil and Ben wouldn't be going home for dinner, Sloane suspected there'd been a lot of texts flying back and forth between her family members that afternoon. Texts to which she, suspiciously, was not privy.

That was it. Tomorrow she was going to find Verona Charles, the town's unofficial matchmaker, and point her toward Adam or Angel. Turnabout was fair play, after all. She just had to get through this dinner and see the last of Jason Till as he drove off for wherever he was headed next.

When she turned to put glasses filled with tea on the table, she found that the other members of her family had already seated themselves. Other than her mom's normal spot, there was one empty chair left. Right next to Jason.

A lot of things could be said about Sloane—she was a hard worker, a loyal friend, determined and liked to help others. She also was really good at paybacks, no matter how long she had to wait to mete them out.

Chapter Five

Sloane had just taken her first bite of the delicious ribs when her mom said, "So, Jason, tell us about yourself."

Her mother sounded like her normal, sweet self, but to Sloane's ears there was no mistaking what this was—one part interrogation and one part highlighting the résumé of a potential son-in-law. She bit her lip to keep from telling her mom to back off.

She tried and failed to deny to herself that she was interested in his answer.

"Not much to tell really," he said. "I'm from Idaho, but while I was growing up I probably spent more time on the road than anywhere. Both my parents were in the rodeo."

Sloane got the image of that tumbleweed in her head again. If she'd thought him not the type to settle down before, here was even more evidence.

"Was your dad a steer wrestler, too?" her dad asked.

"No, he rode bareback. Mom was a barrel racer. Both retired now. My sister and I grew up on the circuit."

The sister who was now a marketing person. "So your sister didn't go into the family business," Sloane said.

Out of the corner of her eye, she saw him glance at her, but she didn't look toward him.

"We both did junior rodeo when we were young, but Shannon didn't want to do it professionally. So she went to college instead."

She had to be imagining things because she thought she heard a hint of envy in Jason's voice. But everything about him said rodeo, just like so many other riders she'd seen roll into town for a weekend, long enough to compete, party at the music hall and do their best to make a local gal fall in love with them.

Well, that sure as heck wasn't happening to her.

"Probably a lot less likely to break her neck in marketing." She winced inwardly, realizing as the words left her mouth that she sounded harsher than there was any reason to be. Was it because his coming back to the ranch for a second day had given her mom more ammunition in her matchmaking efforts?

Still, she was determined to act as if his presence didn't bother her. She wasn't exactly doing a crackerjack job of it at the moment.

"We've always said she has more brains than the rest of us put together," Jason said, easing the layer of tension before she could figure out how to do it herself.

"So what kept you in the rodeo?" Neil's wife, Arden, asked, every inch the reporter looking for answers.

Jason shrugged. "Decent enough at it to make a living. Even made it to the Finals one year."

No one else seemed to notice it, but again there was something in the way Jason answered the question that made her wonder if he wished he'd chosen a different path. She wondered if maybe he didn't even realize it.

"That must have made your parents proud," her mom said.

"Yeah. I think they yelled louder than anyone else there."

As the meal progressed, Sloane listened as first one family member and then another asked Jason questions. It was obvious from his answers that he was close with his family and that he'd had his share of good times on the rodeo circuit. She suspected he wasn't much older than her, so he probably still had a few years of viable competition left. Then she'd bet he'd go back to Idaho and get a ranch next door to his parents' land, spoil his niece and nephew rotten, maybe even start a family of his own.

The image bothered her. But it couldn't be because of Jason. She barely knew the guy. She'd heard women talking about their biological clocks, and she'd always shrugged it off as a bunch of hooey. But had hers just made its first tick?

Oh, for heaven's sake, even her brain was working against her best interests. Though Jason managed to turn the conversation away from himself several times, her family always found a way to shift it back toward him or, even worse, her. By the time they were all done eating, she felt as if her nerves were about to pop like a cork in a champagne bottle.

Just as she believed she was on the verge of being free of the forced togetherness, her mom delivered to the table her famous chocolate cake.

"Oh, you're in for a treat," Ben said to Jason.

Angel leaned toward Sloane's left side. "Mom's not playing."

Sloane slowly turned her head to face her sister. "This is all your fault," she said under her breath, quietly enough that the conversation around the table kept her words from being broadcast to everyone within earshot.

To Sloane's right, she heard Jason's long *mmm* of appreciation that told her he'd just taken a bite of the cake. When she noticed Neil watching her from across the table, she pulled out all the stops to hide how much the sound of that *mmm* made her feel odd and tingly inside.

"So, Jason, where are you off to next?" she asked as casually as she could manage.

"New Mexico."

"Long drive."

"Yeah, I'm used to it though."

"Doesn't it get old?" her mom asked. "I'd think you'd want to settle down at some point."

Sloane couldn't help staring at her mom. Could the woman be any more obvious?

Jason didn't answer immediately. Sloane glanced at him to see he was wiping chocolate icing away from his mouth.

No, don't look at his mouth.

"Rodeo life can't last forever," he said.

Well, that was a rather nonanswer answer, wasn't it? She couldn't tell if he was trying to avoid any sort of commitment or if he really hadn't thought about what came after he became too old or injured to jump off horses and wrestle steers anymore. She supposed he wasn't the only rodeo cowboy not to look any further into the future than the next competition.

Most people had to put a bit more planning and thought into their lives. Sure, rodeo competitors chasing a spot in the Finals had to do some planning along the way. Some probably even already had ranching operations they helped run when not competing, but there were a fair number who had a bit of vagabond about them, too.

"But I figure I have a few years left in me," Jason said.

"Do your parents come to see you compete?" Sloane wasn't sure why she asked the question. Maybe it was just as a blocking maneuver to keep her mom or any of the rest of her family from asking something more frustrating.

"Sometimes, when the rodeo is close enough. Dad had a hip replaced, and driving long distances is uncomfortable now. But they still expect a full report after every competition."

"Living vicariously, huh?" Adam asked.

Jason nodded as he scooped up the last bite of cake with his fork. "Yep."

Sloane noticed how he quickly shoved the cake into his mouth. Was he tired of being grilled, no matter how laid-back he seemed?

Though he'd had the option of not accepting her mom's dinner invitation and avoiding all the questioning, she also knew her mom and how she didn't like to take no for an answer when issuing dinner invitations. Sloane suddenly felt as if she needed to throw Jason a life preserver. She pushed back from the table.

"I feel as if I need to walk to Dallas and back after eating all that."

Jason patted his stomach. "You're not kidding."

It hit Sloane too late that she might have just opened herself up to misinterpretation. She hadn't meant it to sound as if she wanted to go for a walk with him. But it was too late to backtrack now. Instead, she stood and started gathering dishes.

"Let me help," Jason said as he stood beside her.

"No need," Sloane said at the same time her mom said, "That's nice of you, Jason."

She was definitely having a talk with her mom once Jason left. Teasing and gentle prodding was one thing. This felt like an all-out matchmaking offensive. Knowing it would just make matters worse, she didn't argue against his help as she carried dirty dishes to the kitchen and began to rinse them off. As she reached to open the dishwasher, Jason assumed her place at the sink. Without a word, he began rinsing dishes and handing them to her.

"Thanks," she said, trying for the same amount of gratitude she would have shown any of her siblings in the same situation.

But Jason wasn't one of her siblings. No, he was a tall, handsome man taking up way too much space beyond the bounds of her comfort zone.

"Least I can do after that meal. I don't think I'll have to eat for a week."

She laughed a little at that. "You forget I grew up with three brothers. My bet is that you'll be hungry again before the night is through."

Her mom entered the kitchen to put away leftovers. As she opened the fridge, she said, "It's almost dark already. Jason, why don't you spend the night here? We have plenty of room now that Ben and Neil have moved out, and I hate the idea of you driving so late."

Okay, this was too much. "Mom, I'm sure Jason has a schedule to keep."

"There's no sense in him spending money on a motel tonight when there are two perfectly good, empty beds here."

Her dad walked into the room and clapped Jason on the shoulder. "You play poker?"

"Some."

"Good enough. It's settled then. We'll get a game going in a while, and you can spend the night and enjoy a big breakfast in the morning before you head out."

Jason glanced at her, and she wondered if she looked as stunned as she felt. Her dad never used to be the type to interfere with his kids' dating decisions. Had the marriage of his two oldest sons changed his view on that hands-off policy? Great, not a single ally in the house.

She realized Jason was still looking at her, so she doubled down on the "I don't care" act and shrugged.

"It's definitely better than anything you'll find along the interstate."

"You all have convinced me. Thank you."

Sloane worried that her parents had the entire night to figure out a way to convince Jason to stay past breakfast. She worried that she didn't mind that idea as much as perhaps she should.

WHEN THE GUYS commandeered the dining room table for their poker game, Sloane took the opportunity to vacate the premises. In one of the few moments no one was watching her, she slipped out the front door and headed to the barn. There wasn't any work left to be done there, but at least she could hear herself think. And the horses weren't likely to care who she did or didn't date.

"Hey there, fella," she said to Hector, a dappled gray that was the friendliest horse on the ranch. She reached over the side of the stall and rubbed his face. "So, what do you think of becoming an artist?"

She'd used the horse art idea as a way to divert the

conversation earlier, but what if it really did work? Some people might be willing to buy a pitiful excuse for art if it was for a good cause. Heck, they did it all the time, didn't they?

Part of her would like to ask Jason's sister for advice on how to set up and run such a fund-raising effort, but she didn't want to give him the impression she was trying to become more tied to his family. In fact, she needed to apologize to him for how her parents and siblings were coming at him from all sides.

Did he really mind it though? If he did, wouldn't he have said thank you and goodbye after dinner instead of agreeing to be an overnight guest? He'd felt obligated to accept the dinner invitation, but availing himself of free lodging was something else entirely. He'd joked about going out with her, but he had to have gotten the message by now that she wasn't interested.

Okay, so not interested was stretching the truth. She just prided herself on having a good, sensible head on her shoulders and a firm grasp on common sense. Getting involved, even for a hot minute, with Jason Till wasn't sensible in any way, shape or form.

The sound of footsteps drew her attention to the open doorway. As Angel walked in, she held up a hand in a "halt" gesture.

"Before you say anything, I'm sorry," Angel said. "I didn't realize my teasing was going to light a bonfire under Mom."

Sloane turned toward her sister, one arm still propped on the front of the stall. "How could you not? Ever since Neil and Ben gave her a double wedding—every mother's dream on steroids—she's been itching to get the rest of us hitched. I don't know about you, but if I ever decide

I want to walk down the aisle, I'd like it to be toward someone of my choosing."

Angel came to stand next to her and let Hector nibble at her fingers. "I guess I didn't realize how serious she was."

Sloane sighed. Chances were their mom wasn't pressuring Angel as much because she'd been through one bad relationship already, and no one wanted to risk her having another, especially not when she had a daughter to consider. But Sloane and Adam...well, they were evidently fair game. Everyone seemed to either be blind to her terrible dating track record or had just convinced themselves she'd simply not found the right person yet. It had been obvious to everyone that she and Tim Bartlett had only enough in common to last a couple of weeks. She'd seen a bit more hope in her mom's eyes when Sloane had dated Jeremy Jarvis for a few months, but Sloane had lost what enthusiasm she'd had for the pairing when she'd caught Jeremy making out with some barrel racer outside the music hall.

Her family's apparent belief that "the one" was still out there for her was one part sweet but ninety-nine parts annoying. They chalked up her dating misses as the kind of duds everyone went through, rather than part of a pattern that had started with the biggest mistake of all. Of course she'd never let on how much Blake's leaving had hurt her, how she often wondered if her radar for decent guys was broken beyond repair. She doubted her family realized the end with Blake had been anything more than a typical high school breakup. Now, evidently, the fact that she was older than Adam, or maybe because her mom had a hankering to be a mother of the bride, Sloane was the winner of the latest round of matchmaking. Oh, joy.

"Just tell her to back off," Angel said. "But don't tiptoe around it."

"So be rude to Mom."

"Not rude, firm. Otherwise she might not realize how much this really bothers you. She might think you're just being your normal stubborn self."

"Gee, thanks."

Angel shrugged. "Just being honest." She scratched between Hector's ears. "So you don't like Jason at all?"

"He's a nice enough guy."

"And handsome."

"He's not totally ugly."

Angel snorted. "Sloane Hartley, queen of terrible compliments."

"Okay, he's good-looking. But also—and this is sort of important—he doesn't live here."

"Give Mom time. She'll have him living here full-time."

Sloane grabbed her sister around the neck and noogied her head, causing Angel to squeal and do her best to wriggle away the same way she had when they were kids.

"Not fair," Angel said as she finally freed herself.

"Always going to be the big sister. Always going to be better at noogieing."

"Just for that, I ought to go back in the house and tell Mom you've fallen madly in love with Jason."

"Do that and a noogie will be the least of your worries."

Angel laughed as she smoothed her mussed hair. "For whatever it's worth, I don't think you enjoying some time with Jason, maybe even going on a date, would be you caving in to Mom's master plan. It might be fun."

But what she feared was that it was the kind of fun that led to too much, too fast and left you wanting more, a *more* you could never have.

Chapter Six

Jason walked out onto the front porch of the Hartleys'
house after the poker game was over. Normally on a
Sunday night he was on some dark highway heading toward wherever he was to compete next. Tonight's home-
cooked meal, lively conversation and laughter made him
a bit homesick. It'd been a while since he'd gone back to
Idaho to visit his family. He needed to find a space in
his schedule to do that. It might require him to rethink
which rodeos he wanted to compete in. But there wasn't
a lot of wiggle room unless he won several big rodeos.

He noticed the light on in the barn and guessed he
might find Sloane there. When he reached the barn, he
found her sitting on a stack of hay bales scrolling on
her phone.

"Trying to book your escape?" he asked as he am-
bled toward her.

She laughed a little at that before looking up. "How
did you know?"

He sank onto the hay bales beside her. "Could have
been when I thought you were going to shoot lasers out
of your eyes at your mom."

"Yeah, I'm not the world's best at hiding my feelings."

"What? I hadn't noticed."

She lifted an eyebrow at him.

"Listen, I wasn't lying when I said I'd like to go out with you, but I didn't know your family would react like that."

She lowered the phone to her lap. "You just happened to come along when Mom is in matchmaking mode. Neil and Ben got married not that long ago, so she still has wedding on the brain. You should run while you're safely outside the house."

"And miss a real breakfast in the morning? I don't think so."

Plus, while Diane would be disappointed if she was looking forward to another wedding, he wasn't in any hurry to leave Sloane behind. Maybe it was because she didn't seem interested in snagging herself a rodeo cowboy. He didn't have to guard against making a poor decision and getting himself in a bad situation like he'd seen some guys do. Not that he couldn't imagine spending a night with Sloane. That was actually pretty easy to imagine. But he was certain she wouldn't have any "gotcha" motive if that ever happened. He hadn't been a monk throughout the years, but he was careful. His parents had drilled that necessity into both him and Shannon from an early age because his dad's best friend had fathered not one but two kids with women he'd met at rodeos, women he could barely remember. The last thing he wanted was to father a kid with someone he barely knew. Talk about something that would rob him of the focus he needed to have on his work. A little fun was one thing, a lifetime of commitment quite another.

Sloane shook her head at him. "I hope Dad and my brothers took all your money."

"Quite the opposite." He reached into his pocket and pulled out a wad of dollar bills. "It looks like more than it is, but I want you to have it."

She leaned away from him, her features knitted in confusion.

"For the camps," he said. "Your dad said you hope to expand. I'd like to make a contribution."

"You can't buy a date with me."

"Not trying to. I'm hoping you'll go out with me because of my irresistible charm."

"And your obvious modesty?"

He smiled. "Of course."

She laughed. "This probably works for you most of the time, doesn't it?"

"It's hit-and-miss."

He extended the money to her. "Take it. Use it however will help the most."

"I can't take your money. I'm sure you could use it."

"Consider it payment for my meals and room for the night."

"Jason—"

He captured her hand and placed the bills in her palm. "Just take it. Not for you. For the kids."

She looked at him as if she was trying to decipher something written in a foreign language. "Thank you."

"Wish I could do more." The money he won went back into travel, rodeo fees, living expenses. Any left after that he sent to his parents. Unless you made it big, the rodeo life didn't really offer a good retirement plan, and their ranch was small potatoes compared to the ones he'd seen here in Texas.

"You helped a lot this weekend."

He leaned against the empty stall behind them. "You

would still have done all the same things even if I hadn't been here."

"Yeah, but an extra set of hands helped. And the kids liked you."

"They were sweet kids. Found myself wishing I could do more for them."

"I know that feeling."

"How did you get started doing the camps?"

She shrugged. "Heard about some similar programs. Seemed like a good idea. We're all adopted, so helping out kids is a natural fit, I guess."

He was curious what Sloane's story was, why she was adopted, but that was way too personal a thing to ask about considering they'd only met two days ago.

"Speaking of the kids," she said. "What did you give Phoebe right before she left?"

"A necklace, just a leather string with a little wooden horseshoe on it. Mom gave it to me when I started riding professionally for good luck. Thought maybe Phoebe could use it more than me."

"That was...nice of you."

He grinned. "What can I say? I'm a nice guy."

"And you ruined it."

"Darn. I was hoping I was closer to getting you to say yes to going out with me."

"Dude, why are you trying so hard? You'll be long gone tomorrow."

"Maybe not. I have time to stick around for a day or two."

Sloane suddenly got to her feet and walked across the alley, then turned to face him. "Why would you want to do that?"

Excellent question.

He stayed where he was, respecting the physical distance she'd put between them. "Told you. I'm angling for a date."

"But why? You don't even know me really."

"Isn't that what dates are for, to get to know each other?"

"I doubt we'd get to know each other very well on a single date." She braced her hands against her hips and took a couple of steps farther into the barn before turning back toward him. "Sorry. I don't mean to be rude. I just don't think it's a good idea."

"Because your family is pushing for it or because you aren't interested?"

Sloane opened her mouth as if to answer, but nothing came out.

"You wouldn't be giving in if it's your choice," he said.

Sloane crossed her arms and stared at him for a long moment. "You're certainly persistent."

"Is it going to pay off?"

"Will you take no for an answer?"

"Probably not." When he realized how that sounded, he smiled in the hope it lessened any possible "I'm a stalker" vibes he might have unintentionally put out there.

"What happened to it being my choice?" she asked.

"It's still your choice. But I might choose to keep asking until I become so adorable you can't keep saying no."

"I'd only have to outlast you for a max of forty-eight hours."

Jason stretched his legs out and crossed his ankles. "I guarantee it'll be more fun if you don't."

When she shook her head, he figured he'd pushed it as far as he could. He'd spend the night, enjoy his breakfast so he didn't offend Mrs. Hartley, then go pick up his horse and trailer from the fairgrounds and hit the road.

"Fine, on one condition."

"Okay," he said, honestly surprised she'd finally agreed.

"Don't say anything to my family, and we go somewhere away from Blue Falls."

"Sneaky. I like it."

"Don't make me regret my decision."

He put up his hands, palms out. "You pick the place since you're familiar with the area."

She shook her head a little. "I can't believe I agreed to this."

"Hey, look at it this way—if the date is terrible, you'll never have to see me again."

"You make a valid point."

He smiled again, determined that their date was going to be anything but terrible.

"ARE YOU SURE you don't want any more pancakes?"

Sloane glanced toward the table where Jason was waving off her mom's offer of what had to be the tenth pancake.

"Mom, there is food between here and New Mexico," she said.

"You know I don't let anyone go away from my table hungry."

"Well, no danger there," Sloane said as she poured herself a second cup of coffee. She was going to need the caffeine after a night of very little sleep. Knowing Jason was just down the hallway, probably sleeping in nothing more than his underwear, had caused her to toss and turn and imagine way too many naughty scenarios.

Almost as soon as she'd gone to bed she'd started questioning why she'd allowed Jason to convince her to go out with him. It wasn't as if it could lead anywhere.

Since when did a date have to lead anywhere beyond a few hours of fun? She'd proven she was awful at picking someone who could lead to anything more. From the moment she'd met Jason, she'd for some reason been overthinking everything he said, everything he did. She needed to just chill, go on the date and relax. When Jason left, she'd get back to her normal life. And her mom would hopefully get back to hers and stop trying to take Verona Charles's job away from her.

As Jason pushed back from the table and stood, Sloane turned to look out the window so she wouldn't stare at him. The more she was around the man, the more her attraction to him grew. If her mom got any hint of that at all… Well, best if that didn't happen.

"Thank you so much for all the great food and for letting me stay here last night," he said to her mom. "But I should be heading out."

"So soon?"

"Yes, ma'am."

"Well, you're welcome here anytime. Isn't that right, Sloane?"

"Sure." She walked the fence between not sounding rude and not sounding too enthusiastic or interested. She schooled her features and turned toward them. "Thanks for coming out and talking to the kids."

"No problem. I enjoyed it. Good luck with your camps."

She nodded while trying to ignore the knowing gleam

in his eyes. If he wasn't careful, her mom was going to figure out something was up.

"Well, I better get to work, too. Good luck on the rest of your season."

"Thanks."

Sloane poured half the coffee down the drain, quickly rinsed the cup and exited through the back door. She went straight to the barn to tackle the morning chores. She was just letting the last of the horses out of the stalls so she could clean them when she heard Jason's truck start and then head down the driveway. Now that he was leaving the ranch, she considered texting him to cancel their date. But a voice spoke up from somewhere in her brain, telling her that she was being ridiculous.

It was one date, for heaven's sake. Jason was nice, funny and good-looking. And her family wouldn't even know about the date. So she had no reason to be so amped up about it, right?

"Need some help?" her mom asked as she entered the barn.

"Nah, I'm good."

"Shame to see Jason leave. He's a nice man."

"Who has to make a living like the rest of us."

Her mom propped her forearm along the top of one of the stalls. "Did you have a problem with him?"

"No."

"Then why did you seem to have your hackles raised every time he was around?"

Well, she wouldn't get a better opening than that. "It wasn't him, Mom. It was you."

"Me?" She sounded genuinely surprised.

"Ever since Neil and Arden got together, you have made it your mission to get us all married off."

"I'm not allowed to want my children to be happy?"

"I didn't say that. But we ought to be able to decide what or who makes us happy."

"A little nudge here and there doesn't hurt. It worked for Ben and Mandy."

"A nudge is one thing. A giant shove at every turn is something different." Sloane paused at the change in her mom's expression, the fading of the twinkle in her eyes. "Listen, I know you mean well. But you also know that if someone tries to push me into something, it just means I'm going to fight against it all the harder."

Her mom sighed. "He just seemed like such a nice guy. And he was good with the kids, which I thought would be important to you."

"From what little I know, you're right. He's a decent guy. Maybe he'll even make someone a good husband one day. But it's not going to be me. And I doubt he'll settle anytime soon. You heard him. Rodeo runs in that family's blood."

"There are plenty of rodeo riders who are married."

"Yeah, but that's got to be hard, don't you think? You either have to travel with them for months at a time or stay home and rarely see them. If I ever decide to be with someone, I'm sure as heck not chasing them all over the country. My life is here."

The same as it had been when Blake decided his wasn't.

Her mom didn't respond for several seconds, but then she nodded. "Understood."

For the next several minutes, they worked silently side by side to get the barn chores done in half the normal time. When her mom said she had some things to do in the house and left, Sloane felt as if she'd wounded her somehow. And the fact that she was actually going out with Jason and not telling her made Sloane feel even worse.

Maybe she wouldn't end up going. She still hadn't figured out a suitable excuse for leaving for the evening, at least not one that wouldn't send up red flags. Her mom had agreed to back off, but that didn't mean her ornery siblings would.

She mentally argued with herself all day about whether the date was a good idea. By the time late afternoon came, she was convinced the two sides of the argument were going to start throwing punches in her head.

Fate was finally smiling on her when she returned to the house to find it empty. Her dad, Neil and Adam were still out on the ranch working. Ben was busy in his saddle shop. Angel had gone to a parent-teacher conference with Julia. And, best of all, her mom had left a note on the dining room table that she'd gone into town to meet with Mandy's mom about plans for their next farmers' market.

Before one of the moving parts of her family made a reappearance, she hurried through her shower and changed clothes. She refused to dress up. That would signal that she was putting too much importance on this date. She was just going to go out, have dinner, maybe laugh a little, then call it a night. Everyone deserved a break every once in a while.

Her luck ran out the moment she walked back into the kitchen to leave a note on the table that she wouldn't be home for dinner. She found Ben leaning against the counter munching on a bowl of popcorn.

"Where you off to in such a hurry?"

"I'm not in a hurry."

"Where are you *not* in a hurry to get to?"

Her mind fumbled a bit over the reason she'd concocted. She just hoped he didn't notice. "Going into Austin to meet with some people about ideas for growing the camps."

"Pretty casual outfit for a meeting."

"Since when are you the fashion police?"

He gestured toward her with a piece of popcorn. "Since I think you're going out on a date with Jason Till."

Somehow she managed not to react with the shock she felt. How in the world had he figured that out?

"Well, that would be difficult since he left for New Mexico this morning."

"Did he?"

Sloane leaned her hip against the edge of the table. "Yes. What is up with you?"

He shrugged. "Just found it interesting when I saw Jason pulling his trailer through town about an hour ago, and that he wasn't heading toward the interstate."

Oh, crap. "Maybe he likes to go back roads or something."

"Come on. I get why you'd hide this from Mom. But why me?"

Sloane huffed in disbelief then pointed toward the popcorn in his hands. "Oh, I don't know, perhaps because you treat my life as entertainment."

"I seem to remember you dishing it out when I was dating Mandy."

And now it was coming back to bite her in the butt.

Ben wore a satisfied smile as he dramatically tossed a piece of popcorn into his mouth. The look in his eyes told her that there was no use denying the truth. Instead, she jabbed her forefinger in his direction.

"If you breathe one word of this to anyone, especially Mom, I will find a way to make you regret it. And you know I can do it, too."

His smile widened before he mimed zipping his lips.

"And it's no big deal," she said.

"Big enough that you're hiding it."

"I don't want to get Mom's hopes up when it's just a single casual date. I used to be able to go out and have some fun without her hearing wedding bells. Having to sneak around as if I'm a teenager is partly your fault."

"Neil started it."

How many times had she heard that sentence as they'd all been growing up? She rolled her eyes and turned to leave the room. "Remember what they say about paybacks."

The entire drive into Blue Falls, Sloane hoped she didn't pass her mom on the road. She actually breathed a sigh of relief when she reached the turn that led off through the Hill Country toward the small town of Poppy. It wasn't as big as Blue Falls, but it was in a really pretty spot along the Frio River. And she wouldn't know every third person who walked past their table at dinner like she would in Blue Falls.

As she weaved her way along the curvy, hilly road, she gave herself a much-needed pep talk. If she was going through with this date, she might as well enjoy it. If Ben spilled the beans, she'd deal with it later. It wouldn't do her any good to worry about it now. And maybe they would talk about the camps, so her story wouldn't be a complete lie.

She slowed down as she drove into the outskirts of Poppy. The town was home to only about five hundred people, give or take, but it was a little gem that tourists were beginning to discover. Though it boasted only one street of businesses, a lot of them antiques stores, it seemed there was something new every time she managed to visit. Its location on the beautiful Frio River was its biggest selling point. When Texas got as hot as blue blazes, people flocked to the cold, clear swimming holes and enjoyed leisurely floating down the river in tubes. The previous summer, someone had opened a sort of drive-in restaurant beside the river for tubers. They didn't even have to get out of the water for their burgers and fries.

Sloane drove past the line of antiques stores, the tiny town hall and the lot that was ringed with food trucks surrounding an area filled with brightly colored picnic tables. At the far end of town, she pulled into the parking lot for Taste Bud's, a barbecue place overlooking the river. Bud Tanner was a huge mountain of a man who lived and breathed making what many claimed was the best damn barbecue in Texas. He'd also had a rough childhood, so when he'd read about her camps, he'd donated some barbecue meals for the kids a few times.

When she spotted Jason's truck, her heart suddenly started beating a lot faster. She tried to slow its pace, but it ignored her efforts. If she was smart she'd turn around and go back home. Her body didn't normally react this way when she went out on a "casual date." The truth was she liked Jason, probably too much considering their short acquaintance. And she'd experienced an immediate physical attraction, one that had only strengthened each time she saw him. If he were local or sticking around, she might be inclined to see where things went with him, perhaps even daring to hope to break her dismal dating streak. But he wasn't.

She needed to remember that. Tonight would be no more than a fun evening out without the scrutiny and pressure of her family before they went their separate ways.

Even telling herself that didn't seem to have any effect on her rapid pulse. She took a long, deep breath and got out of her truck. She'd traded her boots for cooler sandals, but her jeans and T-shirt were similar enough to what she normally wore that she was confident she didn't appear as if she'd tried too hard to impress Jason. So she'd left her hair down and put on some makeup. That was just so she didn't look as if she'd gone straight from the barn to dinner. At least that's what she told herself until she spotted Jason. When she saw how well he cleaned up in obviously newer jeans and a blue button-down, she admitted he looked yummy enough to eat. And that maybe she'd made the little extra effort with her own appearance hoping he'd think the same about her.

Chapter Seven

"You showed," Jason said as he crossed the waiting area to where she stood just inside the door. "I figured I had a fifty-fifty chance of being stood up."

"I won't lie. I thought about it. I would have at least texted you though."

He smiled. "Considerate of you."

Did the man have any inkling how annoyingly handsome he was when he smiled like that?

"Welcome to Taste Bud's," a young woman said as she returned to the hostess stand. "Would you like inside or outside seating?"

Jason gestured to Sloane, indicating the decision was up to her.

"Outside, please."

"Right this way."

The hostess seated them at one of the tables at the edge of the deck overlooking the river. Tall cypress trees provided shade, and the gurgle of the gently flowing river eased some of her anxiety. She wasn't normally an anxious person, but since the moment she'd met Jason something about him had kept her on edge. And yet here she sat across from him willingly.

"You look nice," he said once they were seated with menus in hand.

"Yes, as you can tell I put in a ton of effort."

"You didn't have to put in any on my account. You're pretty even when you're mucking out stalls."

"Laying it on a little thick, aren't you?" She didn't look up from her menu even though she'd known what she wanted before leaving Blue Falls.

"I'll have you know I'm as honest as they come."

She placed the menu on the table and met his gaze. "Okay, then, tell me why you were so determined that I go on this date with you."

"You mean other than the fact that you're beautiful, give to children in need and have an interesting sense of humor? I can't think of a thing."

Her traitorous body heated because he thought she was beautiful, but she didn't let it show. "*Interesting* sense of humor, huh?"

He leaned forward. "It's got bite. I like that."

She refused to think about biting and Jason in the same train of thought for fear some of those naughty images that had paraded through her brain the night before might return. *Oops, too late.*

Thank goodness, the waitress showed up then to divert Jason's attention long enough for Sloane to get her mind set on a different path.

"What can I get for you?" the waitress asked.

"Wings and potato salad."

After Jason ordered brisket and the waitress left, he laughed a little. "Texas ranch girl orders chicken wings."

"Hey, don't knock the wings. They're out of this world."

"Now, there's a gal who knows what she's talking about."

She knew that deep voice. "Hey, Bud."

"Don't just 'Hey, Bud' me. Get up and give me a hug."

She did, and when his big arms enveloped her she remembered just how small Bud Tanner could make her feel. Considering she was five foot nine, that wasn't an easy feat. Done with the hug, he took a step back and directed his attention toward Jason.

"I see you brought me a new customer," he said.

She'd come to Poppy to avoid seeing people she knew, but she wasn't worried about Bud. He wasn't the type to go blabbing about other people's business.

"Bud Tanner, this is Jason Till. He rode in the Blue Falls Rodeo this weekend and came out to talk to the campers about what rodeo life is like."

Bud extended his hand for a shake, which Jason accepted.

"Well, anyone helping out with those kids is good people in my book." Bud kept his obviously firm grip on Jason's hand. "At least he better be if he's out with this fine lady."

Sloane swatted one of Bud's meaty arms. "You know good and well I can take care of myself. And I've already got a dad and three brothers. That's about as much protector testosterone as I can handle."

"Sorry, hon. It's what I do."

"How about you protect me from starving to death by going and hurrying up our order?"

Bud barked out a laugh as he finally released Jason's hand. "Maybe I should be protecting him from you."

She smiled. "Maybe."

When Bud headed back toward the kitchen, she looked over at Jason to find him grinning at her.

"What?"

"So I might need protection from you, huh? Sounds as if this date might get really interesting."

"Yeah, try anything I don't like and I'll toss you into the river."

"Okay, so sticking to things you like." He wiggled his brows. "And what might that be?"

A few things rushed through her mind, none of which she was willing to say out loud. And all of which were incredibly bad ideas.

"The usual—puppies, ice cream, any movie with Chris Hemsworth in it."

He laughed at her response before taking a drink of his soda as he looked at her with a curious expression. "So how long have you been holding the camps?"

She hadn't really thought about what they'd talk about during dinner, but the camps seemed a safe enough topic. "Couple of years. Only had one the first year, three in the second. This weekend's was the first one of this year."

"How much do you want to grow it?"

"Eventually? At least one camp a month, and be able to bring out more kids each time. That's the dream anyway. It'll have to be a slow build though. I refuse to take money away from the ranch's bottom line, so I pick up odd jobs when I can. Mom and I coupon and fill out rebates to pay for the food to feed the kids. We get occasional donations, like Bud donating barbecue. I applied for a couple of grants, but nothing has come through yet."

"I'll talk to Shannon and see what she says."

"You don't have to do that."

"I know, but she'll love it. She's a good soul."

"Must run in the family." For a moment she thought maybe that answer was too revealing, but then she realized there was nothing wrong with telling that kind of truth. She wanted to see more kindness and giving in the world, so encouraging and complimenting it seemed like a wise thing to do.

"Thank you." There was no teasing in his words this time.

She glanced toward the river and saw a couple of colorful kayaks floating by.

"Looks like fun," Jason said.

"Yeah, though I'm more of a tuber myself. Way more relaxing."

"I've never done that."

"Not exciting enough?"

"Not enough time."

"Seems you make time for things when you want to."

"That I do." The suggestive grin he shot her way caused her skin to tingle as if she were about to be struck by lightning.

The waitress arrived with their food, giving Sloane a few moments to try to come up with a new topic of conversation. Anything but how Jason looked more delectable than anything on the menu.

"Can I ask you a personal question?" he asked as soon as the waitress left the table.

"You can ask. No guarantee I'll answer."

"Fair enough. I know you and your brothers and sister are adopted. Are any of you birth siblings?"

She shook her head as she picked up one of the wings

from the basket in front of her. "No. All from different families, adopted at different times."

"That says a lot about your parents."

"They're the best kind of people. Mom wasn't able to have kids and they wanted someone to pass the ranch down to. They like to joke that adopting kids was kind of like eating potato chips. You can't stop with just one."

"Do you mind me asking about your background?"

She experienced the pang of loss she always did when she thought about her early years. "Not much to tell. I lost my parents when I was young and didn't have any other family."

"What happened?"

This was pretty heavy first-date conversation, but it surprised her that she didn't mind. Resist him all she wanted, he was still easy to talk to.

"My mom died when I was two, so I don't remember her. Of the flu of all things." And thus why she never missed a flu shot and wouldn't allow her family to either. "Dad…" She swallowed, feeling the ache in the part of her heart reserved for him. "He had lung cancer."

"I'm sorry I brought up bad memories." Jason reached across the table and wrapped his hand around hers, giving it a supportive squeeze.

"It's okay." And it was. While a part of her would always miss the parents who brought her into the world, sometimes it was nice to talk about them. But she'd always been hesitant to do so with her adoptive parents. Though she had no doubt they wouldn't mind, some part of her feared hurting them and they didn't deserve that.

"What was your dad like?"

She smiled at a memory that sprang to mind. "He was the best. I remember one time—I must have been five because it was before he got sick—I climbed up this tree in our backyard only to discover I was too scared to make my way back down. Dad climbed up and sat beside me for a while, pointing out things all over the neighborhood that we couldn't see from the ground. When it started to get dark, he put me on his back and climbed down. He always made me feel safe."

For a long time after she'd arrived at the ranch, feeling safe had seemed like something that only existed in her past. In her six-year-old brain there'd been a lot of fear that either she or everyone around her would die.

"Gradually, my adoptive parents made me feel safe, too, and I stopped thinking about them as 'adoptive' parents. They were just my parents."

Jason nodded. "That's how my dad has always thought of his parents, too."

"He's adopted?"

"Yeah, when he was a newborn. He never knew who his birth parents were though, so it was different than having known them and losing them."

The simple fact that his dad was adopted created a feeling of connection with Jason she hadn't expected. A warmth built in her chest, starting to melt the invisible barrier she'd erected between them.

"Is that why you agreed to come speak to the kids?"

The mischievous grin came back. "Nah, that had more to do with a certain pretty blonde."

She laughed off his compliment, trying to hide how it caused an entirely foreign giddiness to rise up within her.

"I hate to think of how many women have fallen for that line."

"None. It's brand-new." He watched her for a long

moment. "Also, it's not a line. I like you, Sloane Hartley. Get used to it."

He said it as if he'd be around beyond this one night. And in that moment, she wished he would.

But she'd learned a long time ago that wishing for something didn't make it come true. The fact that her thoughts were even traveling in that direction was so surprising that she didn't truly know what to make of them. Was her mom's talk of her finding love and starting her own family getting to her? It wasn't as if she hadn't had the occasional thought herself, but a passing thought was all it had ever been, since there was no one in her life to fill the missing part of that picture.

She had to remind herself there still wasn't anyone in the picture. Even if she and Jason had a fabulous time tonight, he would be gone tomorrow. It was possible she might see him again, maybe in a year when the Blue Falls Rodeo fit into his schedule again. That thought caused an ache in her chest.

As they ate, she told him more about the camps and life in Blue Falls.

"Sounds a bit like where I'm from, about an hour outside of Boise. It's not as big as Blue Falls though." He made a circular motion with his finger in the air. "More like Poppy. I never could get away with anything."

"But I'm betting you tried."

"Don't all little boys?"

"Hey, it's not only the domain of boys. Angel and I engaged in our fair share of mischief, too." She smiled. "Only we were better at not getting caught."

When they finished their meals, the waitress left them the dessert menu to peruse.

"Do you want anything?" he asked.

"Heck, yeah. You convinced me to go on this date. You're totally buying me dessert."

"Is it so bad that you have to have cake to get through it?"

"Not just cake, but ice cream, too."

"Wow."

She laughed at his feigned offense and decided to reveal a little more truth than she was honestly comfortable sharing. "You're not that bad. I could even skip dessert."

"Oh, no," he said with a wave. "Now I want about half an apple pie."

She tossed her wadded-up napkin at him, and he reflexively batted it away—right into the side of the head of the woman sitting at the next table.

"Oh, I'm sorry," Jason said at the woman's look of annoyance.

Sloane covered her mouth but couldn't totally hide the snort of laughter, especially when Jason shifted his gaze back to her and gave her an "eek" expression.

"How about we find dessert elsewhere?"

"I don't know. I think I might like to see you squirm," she said.

"I was wrong about you. You're actually evil."

She laughed, drawing another annoyed look from the couple at the adjacent table. "Come on. I know a place."

Jason tossed enough money on the table for the bill, then they headed for the exit. The moment his hand rested against her lower back, her entire body woke up as if she'd been walking around half asleep. Was it possible some part of her actually wanted what her mother had been pushing her toward?

She had to remind herself again that it didn't matter. Jason was leaving in a matter of hours. Why did that fact keep trying to wander off and make her believe this was anything more than one night away from work and responsibility?

"So where to?" he asked as soon as they stepped outside.

"This way." She headed for the sidewalk that led back into the part of town she'd passed through earlier.

"Is there apple pie at the end of this jaunt? Because I now have apple pie on the brain."

"Something even better."

"Yeah?"

The suggestive way he said it had her imagining pulling him into the dark, wooded area along the river and satisfying her curiosity about what it would feel like to have his hands on more of her body than just her lower back. Instead, she shook her head.

"Men. You're all alike."

"I sure hope that's not true. I know some real asses."

When they reached the ring of food trucks, they crossed the street. She headed straight for a bright lime-green truck covered with painted cacti and Rosita's in red cursive along the side.

"This place has the best sopaipillas you've ever put in your mouth." She requested two orders and plunked down the money before Jason could retrieve his wallet.

"I should be paying for those."

"Says who?"

"Tradition. Chivalry. Good manners."

She waved off all of those. "Do I seem like the kind of woman to be stuck on tradition to you?"

"I feel as if there's no safe answer to that, so I'm staying quiet."

"Hey, maybe you're smarter than I gave you credit for." She handed him his sopaipilla covered in cinnamon sugar and honey.

They sat at a picnic table and she watched as Jason took the first bite of his sopaipilla. The way he closed his eyes, licked his lips and made a deep sound of appreciation caused those naughty thoughts to come roaring back again. Thoughts that involved Jason in considerably fewer clothes, a large fluffy bed and no one else for miles around.

Okay, this was normal. She was a heterosexual woman and Jason was one hell of a sexy man. His sense of humor and the way he'd been with the kids made him damn near irresistible. Honestly, it was a miracle she hadn't jumped him already.

She took a huge bite of her own sopaipilla so she could pretend any sort of appreciative noise she might make was because of the pastry and not because a part of her was having thoughts about crawling across the table and tackling him.

"That's it," Jason said as he wiped honey away from the edge of his mouth. "I'm never leaving Texas."

She knew it was an exaggeration, but she couldn't deny that she liked the idea of him sticking around more than she should. A reality check hit her like a runaway horse as she finished the last of her sopaipilla. She wiped her mouth with her napkin and balled it in her hand. Well, tonight had been fun while it lasted. While she'd allowed it to last.

"I should be getting home."

Jason's expression was devoid of humor when he asked, "Did I say something wrong?"

"No. Just have a long day tomorrow." No longer than

any other, but it sounded like a plausible excuse to take her leave. She stood, probably too suddenly judging by the surprised expression on Jason's face.

He wiped his mouth and fingers quickly with a napkin and started to gather their trash.

"You don't have to leave," she said. "Sounds as if you might like a second helping."

He lifted an eyebrow at her, then tossed the trash in the nearest can. "Sitting here eating pastries alone wasn't exactly what I had in mind for tonight."

Her pulse jumped throughout her body as if his words had floored its accelerator. "What did you have in mind?"

Did she really want to know? Did she trust herself to know and resist?

As they headed toward the sidewalk, he glanced over at her and took her hand, entwining his fingers with hers. "Something like this."

She didn't know whether to pull away or allow herself to enjoy the feel of his warm, strong, work-roughened hand against hers. Some part of her brain must have decided on the latter because they walked hand in hand down the sidewalk. It was such a simple thing, holding hands, and yet she couldn't remember when she'd last done it. To her, it had always meant more than a hug or even a romantic dinner, sometimes even more than a kiss, and yet here she was holding hands with a man she'd known all of three days. And if she was being honest, it felt good. Really good.

So good that it no doubt was a bad idea. A really bad idea.

Chapter Eight

Jason wasn't entirely sure prolonging his date with Sloane was a good idea because he had a weird feeling in his middle that there was something fundamentally different about spending time with her. Dates for a guy who lived his life on the road like he did usually involved some dancing, laughter, some making out and even occasionally a trip back to his motel room, though he was nowhere near the ladies' man that Bo was.

But what common sense he possessed told him that if he tried that route with Sloane, she really would toss him in the river. And he wouldn't blame her. Though he'd known her only a few days, he firmly believed Sloane deserved better than a one-night stand. Considering he was leaving the next day, he probably shouldn't even be holding her hand. But that simple act made him feel light and full in a way he'd not experienced before. That, in and of itself, should tell him to end the evening. Instead, he veered down a path that led to the river.

They'd only walked a few feet down the path alongside the river when Sloane stopped suddenly and pulled her hand out of his. She took a couple steps away before turning to face him.

"You need to know that I'm not one of those women

who hang around rodeos hoping to snag herself a cowboy to get lucky with."

He crossed his arms and stared back at her. "Did I give you the impression I thought that?"

She gestured at their surroundings. "You insisted on this date. Now we're walking along in near darkness holding hands."

"And that makes you assume I'm planning to drag you off to have my wicked way with you?"

She shifted her weight from one foot to the other and diverted her gaze toward the river. "I didn't say that."

"But you seem suspicious of my motives. Has it occurred to you that maybe I just like you?"

She shrugged as if she either didn't know or was uncomfortable with whatever answer had formed in her mind.

"I'm aware I'm leaving tomorrow and that you're not the type of woman to go for a rowdy night of sex followed by a sayonara the next morning."

She shot him a look that almost seemed offended. Women. He hadn't met one yet he fully understood, not even his own mother and sister. He liked women, just didn't get them.

"We can enjoy the rest of the evening or end it right now, your call," he said.

She watched him for a moment, then spun away and walked farther down the pathway.

Well, he guessed he had his answer.

But then she stopped in front of a bench, stood still for a moment before sinking slowly onto the seat facing the river. After a breath of hesitation, he closed the distance between them and sat beside her. For a couple of minutes, they sat in silence and it was actually kind of nice. The sound of the river gently flowing by was peaceful, the kind of peace that couldn't be found even as he drove alone down empty highways. He had the strangest thought that he could sit right here on this bench forever and be happy.

"I'm sorry," Sloane said.

"For?"

"I shouldn't have made that assumption about your intentions."

"No need to apologize. You had a better than average chance of being right."

"I'm glad I wasn't."

"Ouch. I think my ego just shriveled up and died."

She gave a little snort of laughter. "You know darn well I didn't mean anything derogatory about your attractiveness."

"Is that right?" He playfully bumped her shoulder with his own.

She shook her head. "Men."

"You know you love us."

"I don't know. I'm just glad my parents adopted at least one other girl so I wasn't completely drowning in testosterone and body odor all the time."

"Body odor? I'll have you know I even showered for this date."

She sniffed in an exaggerated fashion in his direction. "You don't totally reek."

"Just for that..." He wrapped his arm around her shoulders and pulled her flush against his side.

When she laughed, it sounded more genuine than anything he'd heard from her, so much so that it pulled him up short. She must have sensed the change in him because she met his gaze. He felt her breath catch in the same moment his did.

"Will you throw me in the river if I kiss you right now?"

The barest hint of a smile played at the edge of her lips. "Only one way to find out."

"Time to live dangerously," he said as he skimmed his hand along her cheek until he was cradling the back of her head.

"Says the man who wrestles steers for a living."

The way her words sounded breathless lit a fire in him that he had to rein in enough so he wouldn't devour her.

"Women are way more dangerous," he whispered as he lowered his lips to hers.

His mouth felt like heaven. Any resistance Sloane might have had to allowing things to progress even a moment ago dived into the river and floated away downstream right along with her common sense.

Jason deepened the kiss gradually as if expecting her to pull away at any moment. But, heaven help her, she didn't want to. Her hand slid up his chest, and an unexpected thrill and hunger went through her at the feel of the firmness beneath his shirt.

He pulled her even closer, and she actually moaned in response to the feel of so much of him pressed against her body. Heat rushed through her and made her feel as if she'd never experienced warmth before. It was the sudden thought that she was boarding a runaway train that was on fire that made her think she should pull away. But before she could follow through, Jason lifted his mouth and eased back from her. She didn't know whether to yank him close again or be thankful he had more willpower than she evidently did.

The thought that maybe he hadn't been enjoying their kiss anywhere near as much as she was made her want to berate herself for giving in to physical attraction. Sure, it was strong, but she was stronger. At least she'd thought she was.

Jason took her chin between his thumb and forefinger so she'd look at him. "Don't think I wouldn't like to continue this, but I don't want you to regret anything about me in the morning."

Was he for real? She didn't know whether to be annoyed he thought things would have gone any further than the kiss or appreciate the fact that he was considering her feelings.

"You're assuming I'd even think about you in the morning."

He released her chin but smiled. "Not even a little bit?"

How did he do that, maintain a good attitude even when she acted waspish? Not for the first time, she wondered where that particular part of her personality came from. Her dad certainly hadn't been prone to such behavior. At least he'd never shown it around her. Adults did often hold some of their worst habits in reserve around kids, but she just couldn't imagine her dad lashing out at someone with no real provocation. And the way her dad had always talked about her mom, Sloane didn't think she inherited the trait from her either.

"Sorry. I don't know why I do that." And she sure as heck didn't know why she'd just confessed that to him either.

He shrugged. "I'm not your type."

She immediately opened her mouth to rebut him but somehow managed to stop herself. Maybe it was best to let him think that, considering they were never going to see each other again, and something about the idea of him thinking she was back here in Blue Falls pining for him made her want to snarl. Probably because she loathed the idea that Blake had once made her feel that way and he likely knew it. She'd sworn to herself she'd never be that person again. Maybe that was part of the reason she hadn't found a relationship that really worked in the years since.

Jason's lips formed a mischievous grin that made her laugh unexpectedly, considering the train of thought her mind had been traveling.

"You're rotten," she said.

"You didn't think so a minute ago."

She punched him in the arm, not hard but not softly either. He just laughed and wrapped his arm around her shoulders. Instinct told her to pull away, but she didn't. If this was to be their only time together, she was going to sit here and enjoy what there was left of it.

"That was the best kiss I've had in a long time," he said.

She fought the smile that wanted to take over her entire face. It should sound like a cheesy line, but instead his words rang with a truth that hit her so deeply it stole her breath for a few moments. And she wasn't the kind of gal whose breath was stolen easily.

"It was fair." She couldn't manage to keep a straight face, but at least it was dark now.

"You just keep telling yourself that."

An unfamiliar feeling filled her. Giddiness. She was actually giddy, like some caricature of a teenage girl if the boy she liked even looked at her. Geez, maybe she needed to toss herself in the river.

"Where are you staying tonight?" They'd agreed to keep this date on the down-low, so he wouldn't be coming back to the ranch.

"Probably drive a ways, then catch a few hours' sleep in the truck."

"That seems mighty uncomfortable."

"Little harder than it used to be when I was younger but I manage. Not the first time I've done it."   .

The thought of getting a room for the night with him formed with such clarity in her mind that she couldn't look his direction for fear he'd see the scene, as well.

"Do you ever get tired of life on the road?"

He didn't immediately respond, was in fact quiet so long that she thought maybe he hadn't heard her even though she knew he must have.

"Sometimes."

There was something about the way he said that single word, as if it was a mixture of uncertainty and stunning realization that caused her to turn toward him.

"I mean, toward the end of the season, it's like anyone else who's ready for a vacation."

She wasn't sure that's exactly what he'd meant by his initial response, but she didn't question his explanation. It was possible she was hearing something that wasn't there, though she didn't think so.

"What about you?" he asked. "Ever want to get away from the ranch?"

"I'm not there now."

"That's not what I mean. For longer than a secret date."

Secret date. That made it sound as if she was doing

something bad, a teenager sneaking out to see the wrong kind of boy.

"Not really. I have everything I want right where I am." Sure, the occasional weekend trip was nice, and she could remember enjoying things about living in San Antonio as a kid, but the ranch was her home. There was nothing like watching the sunrise or sunset over what looked like endless pastures. Or seeing the way the kids who came to her camps gradually shed some of the fear and anxiety so many of them carried with them like a second shadow.

"That's good."

She thought she caught a smidge of wistfulness in his voice.

"Do you enjoy what you do?"

"I don't think wrestling steers is something you do if you don't enjoy it. Lots of safer ways to make a living."

Maybe she'd just imagined the hint of doubt she'd thought she heard in his voice. Was some annoyingly needy part of her hoping he was dissatisfied and would stick around? Well, that was selfish, not to mention unwise.

"I really should be getting home," she said. "A rancher's work is never done."

Instead of trying to get her to stay longer, he stood and extended his hand to her. She probably shouldn't take it, but she did anyway. If she only had a few minutes left with him, she wanted to hush the argument in her head and allow herself to enjoy it.

They didn't talk on the way back to their vehicles, and they didn't rush either. Sloane felt as if she was inhabiting someone else's body with a lot of unfamiliar feelings tumbling around inside of her. But if she had to tell the truth, this time with Jason felt good. Really good. So much so that she had to admit she wished it could last all night.

But she still had a grip on enough common sense that she wouldn't allow herself to step across that particular line. That decision proved difficult to stick to when they reached her truck and Jason spun her into his arms and kissed her again. Though she should be backing away, she fell into the kiss as if it were a huge, clear lake and she was on fire. The way she felt as Jason's strong arms pulled her even closer might very well cause her to combust.

Again, Jason was the first one to step away, only slightly.

"I think we better walk away from each other, don't you?"

It was as if he'd somehow read her desire but also her determination not to let things go beyond the point of no return.

"Yeah." Something in the middle of her chest screamed at her to take back that single word, to change her answer. Instead, she said, "I had a nice time tonight. Thanks for convincing me to do this."

Jason cupped her face with one hand and ran his thumb across her cheek in a gesture so gentle her heart flipped. "I'm glad you showed up. I wasn't sure you would."

"Neither was I."

"Am I that scary?"

"No." *Maybe.* "I'm just practical and this is anything but."

"Sometimes practical is overrated."

The way her body was currently humming, she had

to agree. Before she let that idea run amok, she took a couple of steps away from him, gradually ending their contact. She held his hand, slowly sliding her fingers along the length of his until nothing but air touched her hand. She missed the contact immediately, but she didn't allow herself to seek it out again.

"Good luck at your next rodeo and with the rest of the season."

"Thanks."

For a moment she thought he would say something else and found herself desperately wanting to know what it was. But instead of speaking, he opened her door and gave her a smile she feared would take a long time to forget.

Shooting him a quick smile in return, she climbed into the driver's seat. Neither of them said anything else before she closed the door and drove off down Poppy's main street. To her left, over in the darkness, the river rolled on like it always had. Like her life would. An unexpected sadness settled in her heart.

JASON LEANED AGAINST the rear fender of his truck and watched Sloane drive away. What was it about her that made him want to chase her down to steal one more kiss? Yes, she was beautiful, though he wondered if she realized it. She was close with her family just like he was and extended that caring to children who often didn't have families in their lives. All those things were admirable, but she wasn't the first woman he'd met who was kind and giving. Even when she was prickly, he found her so dang attractive he could barely keep his hands to himself.

Maybe it didn't matter why he felt so drawn to her,

only that he was. But even that defied logic and common sense because his life was about chasing a dream—one within his grasp if he kept his focus where it should be. So why in this moment did he have zero desire to get in his truck and head toward the next rodeo?

Because you're not thinking with the head on top of your shoulders at the moment.

Maybe it was as simple as that. He hadn't gotten laid in quite a while, and his hormones were staging a riot. So he climbed behind the wheel, started the engine and drove out of Poppy into the endless darkness of the Texas countryside. And tried not to think about how a woman he'd met three days ago knocked him temporarily off course. How, at the moment, the thought of being with her beckoned to him more than any rodeo ever had.

Chapter Nine

Sloane listened to the pop of gravel under the truck's tires as she drove up the ranch's driveway. Ahead, she could see the flicker of the TV through the house's front window. She should have made the date last longer so everyone would be asleep when she came home. Because how was she supposed to act natural when she entered the house if she could still feel Jason's kisses on her lips?

A part of her blamed him for putting her in this awkward position. She wasn't the type of person to feel jittery and awkward and, ugh, needy, and yet all of those feelings tumbled around inside her as if they were having a party without her consent.

Oh, hell, she was overthinking this whole thing. She parked and got out of the truck as if she hadn't spent the past few hours imagining a near stranger naked and sucking face in the darkness.

As she entered the house, her mom looked up from where she sat alone on the couch with her laptop. The TV had been turned off sometime between when Sloane parked and when she'd stepped inside.

"How was your meeting?" her mom asked.

"Good." Sloane pointed at the laptop. "What are you working on?"

"Creating a Facebook page for the farmers' market. Well, I started it earlier, and we already have over a hundred likes."

Sloane grinned. "You sounding excited about social media is very amusing."

Her mom shrugged. "There's something oddly exciting about seeing that 'like' number go up. And I've already chatted with three people who are interested in taking part in the next one."

"I'm glad you're enjoying it. Let me know if you need help with anything." Since her mom and Mandy's mom started the periodic farmers' market in town, they'd both jumped on the project with impressive enthusiasm, their friendship growing stronger in the process.

Her mom closed her laptop and placed it on the coffee table. "If I don't move now, I may need help getting off this couch. I've been sitting here since after dinner. I think everyone but your sister has gone home or to bed." Her mom yawned. "Obviously, that's where I need to go."

As her mom passed her, she paused to give Sloane a quick kiss on the cheek. Sloane held her breath, hoping her mom couldn't somehow smell Jason on her.

"Good night, girls."

"Good night, Mom," Sloane said at the same time Angel did from where she sat at the dining room table working on her own computer.

As soon as her mom disappeared into her bedroom, Sloane walked into the dining area. "Working or playing?"

Angel for some reason made a sound that indicated she was amused by the question. "Working. How was your date?"

"I—"

Angel held up her hand in a "stop" gesture. "Don't bother."

"I'm going to kill Ben."

Angel grinned. "To be fair, I didn't give him a choice about sharing what he knew. Plus, I already had suspicions. Now, stop avoiding my question and tell me how it went."

Sloane huffed in exasperation before sinking onto the chair opposite her sister. "Don't breathe a word to anyone. It was one dinner, and I'll never see the guy again."

"I wouldn't be so sure about that. That man could barely peel his eyes off you the entire time he was here."

"You're imagining things."

"Nope, pretty dang sure I'm not."

Sloane slid down in the chair and closed her eyes. Maybe talking to her sister about Jason would help her straighten things out in her head.

"I don't know why I agreed to have dinner with him."

"I do. He pushed all your buttons."

Sloane eyed her sister. "My buttons?"

"He was great with the kids, Mom and Dad like him, the guys didn't run him off the ranch and it doesn't hurt that he's hot."

No, it didn't.

"Maybe I'm thinking about the whole thing too much. Everyone needs a night out now and then."

"See, the way you say that tells me that you feel differently about him than anyone else you've ever gone out with."

Sloane considered denying it, but what would be the benefit in that? It seemed Angel had her pegged anyway. It was true she'd not felt this way in a long time, maybe ever. It wasn't the same as with Blake—it couldn't be.

And the other men she'd dated...well, her attraction to Jason wasn't even in the same universe.

"I can't really describe it, not that it matters."

"Of course it matters, maybe more for you than any of us."

"What does that mean?"

Angel scooted her computer to the side and leaned on the table. "You have a comfort zone of people getting close to you. You're great up until someone threatens to cross that invisible line, then you go all quills-out porcupine."

"Wow, nice image."

"Truth hurts, babe."

"Do I come across as bitchy?" She sure hoped not. She couldn't stand bitchy women.

"Not exactly, but there's a definite 'don't mess with me' vibe sometimes." Angel's expression grew more serious. "Part of me understands it. You don't want to be hurt. I totally get that. But it's also lonely if you never let anyone in."

Sloane suspected Angel might be speaking about herself now. But her sister probably wasn't thinking about herself as a cautionary tale. She'd let someone in and it hadn't ended well. They had that in common. Angel was raising a daughter alone as a result of her failed relationship. That so easily could have been Sloane. Thankfully, Julia had aunts and uncles and grandparents around all the time, so Angel wasn't truly alone. But Julia's dad was who knew where.

"I've never thought of myself as lonely. I like my life just the way it is." Except she wasn't totally sure that was true anymore. If it was, why would she have felt such longing around Jason and a pang in her middle as she'd driven away from him?

"You can keep this life and still find someone. Neil and Ben haven't gone anywhere."

"Maybe so, but it won't be Jason."

"You don't know that for sure. Life has an interesting way of steering you down roads you didn't even know existed."

Sloane refused to argue the point any further. Let her sister believe what she wanted. Sloane chose to live in reality, not fantasy.

Thunder rumbled in the distance. Sloane raised her finger in the air, as if pointing to the thunder. "Sounds as if it'll be a good sleeping night, so I'm off to bed." She pushed away from the table and stood.

"Sweet dreams of hunky rodeo cowboys."

Sloane headed for the doorway. "I need to talk to Mom and Dad tomorrow about trading you in for a newer model of little sister. I hear they have ones now that aren't so annoying."

Angel's chuckle followed Sloane out of the room and toward her bedroom. By the time she'd changed into her pajamas, rain had begun to patter on the roof. As she slipped into bed, she seemed powerless to keep her thoughts from drifting to Jason. To the feel of his mouth on hers and how that contact had awakened a desire in her that was one part exciting and one part scary as hell. And really, really stupid. What good did it do to kiss a man she was never going to see again, especially when that kiss still had her body tingling? None at all.

She flipped onto her side and wrapped her extra pillow in the circle of her arms. As she listened to the rain grow in intensity, she wondered where Jason was at that moment. If he was on the road, would he have the sense God gave a potato to pull over and let the worst of the rain pass? She shivered at the image of him driving off into a ditch.

She closed her eyes and shook her head. He'd successfully been driving dark roads between rodeo stops for more than a decade, so he didn't need her worrying about him. And now that he was gone, she needed to shift her thoughts in a different direction. Ways to help the ranch prosper and plans for future camps and how to fund them. Those things and her family were what were important to her, not some passing-through-town cowboy. Not even if his kisses did make her feel more alive than she had ever known was possible.

JASON JERKED AWAKE, a result of what he realized was a loud sound. It took him a few seconds to process where he was—in the cab of his truck—and that the noise had been the horn of an 18-wheeler passing by the rest area where he had pulled over to catch a few winks when he could no longer see the road for the rain.

Judging by the clear blue sky that greeted him now, the rain had passed right along with several hours. He should be much farther down the road, but he'd only managed a couple of hours of driving after leaving Poppy before the weather had forced him to pull off. While he'd waited for the rain to slacken, he'd kept reliving the kisses he'd shared with Sloane. Damn, those had been some good kisses. And he'd been surprised by how much he had wanted to turn around and go right back to Blue Falls. Which, of course, was crazy.

After a quick trip to the men's room inside the rest area, he got back on the road. When a few minutes later he got into line at a fast-food place, his mouth watered not for the biscuit he was about to order but at the memory of the delicious breakfast he'd had at the Hartleys' house. A familial warmth filled their home that made him miss his own family. He'd been oddly comfortable at the Hartleys' table, sleeping in their home, considering he barely knew them.

Comfortable wasn't exactly the word he'd use to describe how he felt with Sloane. Yes, he'd had fun with her, appreciated how beautiful and hardworking and kindhearted she was despite her sometimes prickly nature, but he'd not really been able to relax with her. His entire body had hummed when she was near, urging him to pull her close.

Man, he needed to put more distance between them so that effect wore off soon. He had a job to do, one that required all his concentration and absolutely zero body humming.

He'd only driven a few miles away from the rest area when his phone rang. The first image that popped into his head, along with a jolt of anticipation, was Sloane's face. Good grief, that had to be the fastest case of infatuation ever experienced. But that was all it was, and he just needed time, distance and the distraction of another rodeo to get him past it.

Instead of Sloane's name on the phone's screen, he saw his sister's.

"Hey, sis," he said in answer.

"Hey, I see you did halfway decent this weekend," Shannon said.

His entire family followed rodeo news like other people followed pro football or college basketball.

"Could have done better but had an off night Friday."

"Where are you now?"

"On my way to New Mexico."

YOUR PARTICIPATION IS REQUESTED!

Dear Reader,

Since you are a lover of our books – we would like to get to know you!

Inside you will find a short Reader's Survey. Sharing your answers with us will help our editorial staff understand who you are and what activities you enjoy.

To thank you for your participation, we would like to send you 2 books and 2 gifts – **ABSOLUTELY FREE!**

Enjoy your gifts with our appreciation,

Pam Powers

SEE INSIDE FOR READER'S SURVEY

For Your Reading Pleasure...

We'll send you 2 books and 2 gifts
ABSOLUTELY FREE
just for completing our Reader's Survey!

YOUR READER'S SURVEY
"THANK YOU" FREE GIFTS INCLUDE:
▶ **2 FREE books**
▶ **2 lovely surprise gifts**

PLEASE FILL IN THE CIRCLES COMPLETELY TO RESPOND

1) What type of fiction books do you enjoy reading? (Check all that apply)
- ○ Suspense/Thrillers
- ○ Action/Adventure
- ○ Modern-day Romances
- ○ Historical Romance
- ○ Humor
- ○ Paranormal Romance

2) What attracted you most to the last fiction book you purchased on impulse?
- ○ The Title
- ○ The Cover
- ○ The Author
- ○ The Story

3) What is usually the greatest influencer when you <u>plan</u> to buy a book?
- ○ Advertising
- ○ Referral
- ○ Book Review

4) How often do you access the internet?
- ○ Daily
- ○ Weekly
- ○ Monthly
- ○ Rarely or never

5) How many NEW paperback fiction novels have you purchased in the past 3 months?
- ○ 0 - 2
- ○ 3 - 6
- ○ 7 or more

YES! I have completed the Reader's Survey. Please send me 2 FREE books and 2 FREE gifts (gifts are worth about $10 retail). I understand that I am under no obligation to purchase any books, as explained on the back of this card.

154/354 HDL GLYU

FIRST NAME

LAST NAME

ADDRESS

APT.#

CITY

STATE/PROV.

ZIP/POSTAL CODE

▼ If offer card is missing write to: Reader Service, P.O. Box 1341, Buffalo, NY 14240-8531 or visit www.ReaderService.com ▼

BUSINESS REPLY MAIL
FIRST-CLASS MAIL   PERMIT NO. 717   BUFFALO, NY

POSTAGE WILL BE PAID BY ADDRESSEE

READER SERVICE
PO BOX 1341
BUFFALO NY 14240-8571

NO POSTAGE
NECESSARY
IF MAILED
IN THE
UNITED STATES

They chatted for a few minutes about how he thought he'd fare in the upcoming rodeo, how the kids were doing, the plans for his parents' anniversary party and finally a big project she was working on at the office.

"Speaking of your work, can I ask you a favor?"

"What, you need a website singing your praises or something?"

He snorted at the very idea. "Nope. I met someone who runs camps for underprivileged kids. I actually went out to tell the campers about life in the rodeo during my downtime over the weekend. They're looking for ways to raise funds to expand the camps so they can bring more kids out to their ranch. I said I'd ask you for some ideas."

"What's their budget? Their goals?"

"No idea, other than Sloane wants to expand."

"Sloane, huh? Is there another story I'm not hearing, little brother?"

"Just trying to help out someone doing something good. Thought you'd like the idea." He couldn't let her think there was something romantic going on between him and Sloane. She'd been trying to set him up ever since her wedding when she'd suggested he ask out one of her bridesmaids. It didn't matter that the bridesmaid in question happened to live in Rhode Island and knew as much about rodeo as he did about...well, Rhode Island.

"Okay, I'll stop teasing. Tell me more about this camp."

As he shared everything he knew about Sloane's camps, he was careful to keep his tone neutral and stick to the facts only. There was a part of him that feared Shannon could read his mind through the phone, see everything that he was omitting.

"Sounds like a good program," Shannon said. "When I get a few minutes, I'll brainstorm some ideas."

"Thanks."

"Don't thank me yet. You'll owe me one."

"Why does that sound ominous?"

"Because I'm going to think of a doozy of a repayment."

After telling Shannon he'd text her Sloane's number the next time he stopped, he ended the call. And discovered that having talked with his sister about the camps, his thoughts refused to focus on anything but Sloane. The next time he stopped for gas, he not only texted Shannon but also Sloane to tell her about his conversation with his sister. He knew the latter was just an excuse to contact her, but it couldn't hurt, right? He was putting more and more distance between them, and the subject of his text had nothing to do with their date. Or the way he wished he could kiss her again right now.

Though he needed to get back on the road, he hesitated. He drew the line at staring at his phone, waiting for a response, so he passed a few minutes washing his windshield and checking on Oscar, his horse.

"So, what do you think, fella?" he asked as he scratched Oscar's forehead through the slats in the trailer. "Have I lost my mind?"

Oscar didn't seem to have an opinion one way or the other.

When Jason's phone buzzed in his pocket, his heart gave an extra thump. He didn't need Oscar to confirm what he already knew—Sloane Hartley had somehow managed to take up residence in too much of his head space. Even knowing that, a sense of excitement thrummed through him as he pulled out his phone and checked the text.

You didn't have to do that, but thank you.

You're welcome, he replied. He held his thumbs over the screen, feeling as if he wanted to say something else but didn't know what.

When he got no further response from Sloane, he took that as a sign he shouldn't have needed that he had to stop thinking about her and get his mind back on the right track. Rodeos didn't win themselves, and he needed wins to make it to the Finals.

SLOANE STARED AT her internet browser, debating whether or not to type in the web address that would provide the answer to her nagging question. It was probably best if she didn't indulge her curiosity. Doing so would only prolong her fixation on Jason. Best just to do everything she could to forget he even existed.

Of course, that was hard when she had somehow managed to dream about him every night since their date. A full week of dreams that ranged from their walking hand in hand along the river to things that were a lot more active and required a good deal more energy. She alternated between replaying those dreams in her mind and chastising herself for wasting so much mental energy on someone she'd gone out with once and who was currently somewhere between New Mexico and wherever his next rodeo was to be held.

She placed her fingers on the keyboard but didn't type anything. What could it hurt? After all, he'd helped at the camp and put her in touch with his sister, who had already given Sloane several interesting ideas to think about regarding funding for the camps. Of course, in return Sloane hoped that he did well in competition. And no one would know if she sneaked a peak at the rodeo results from the weekend and the standings.

The keys clicked softly as she typed in the web address. She didn't even have to scroll to see his name. He'd evidently been able to refocus on his regular life easier than she had. She'd caught herself daydreaming more times than she could count in the past week, sometimes nearly getting caught by her family. Jason...well, he managed to go out and win first place in a rodeo like there was nothing else in the world occupying his mind other than getting the best time in his event.

A knock on her half-open bedroom door startled her so much that she slammed her laptop shut without thinking how guilty that made her look. She turned in her chair to see Angel grinning at her.

"Were you looking at half-naked pictures of a certain Norse god again?"

"Busted." She'd a million times rather her sister think she was feeding her celebrity crush than what she'd actually been doing.

"Uh-huh." Angel didn't sound convinced, but thankfully she didn't press the issue.

"Did you need something?"

"Yeah." As Angel walked into the room, Sloane noticed she had her own thin laptop. Angel placed it next to Sloane's on the desk and opened it. "I'm entering a competition at a magazine, and I need to know which picture I should enter."

"What's the prize?"

"Five thousand dollars and the winning image on the cover of the magazine."

The money would be nice, but that kind of exposure for Angel's work could be worth a lot more. "Let me see."

Sloane examined the two images side by side. One was a line of cowboys in silhouette sitting atop an arena fence with the setting sun bathing them in golden-orange light. The other was a close-up action shot of a bull rider that made Sloane feel as if she were riding the bull right along with him.

"These are both great. If you're going for action, definitely this one. But the other has beautiful atmosphere."

"Which one do you think would be unlike anything else entered?"

Sloane sat back in her chair and stared first at one shot then the other. Her sister's talent for capturing not only images but mood and realistic slices of Western life made the decision difficult, but she finally pointed at the silhouette shot. "This one."

"Oh, good. That's the one I liked, too, but I feel as if I can't judge my own work."

"You should trust yourself more."

"That's some advice that could go the other way, too."

"And with that I have work to do." She started to stand but Angel stayed her with a hand on her shoulder.

"You might want to check your email first."

Without further explanation, Angel headed for the door. "Thanks for the help."

Sloane wondered why her sister had suddenly gone cryptic, but for the second time in the past few minutes her curiosity got the better of her and she opened her laptop again and logged in to her email program.

The body of the email didn't contain any text, making Sloane scrunch her forehead in confusion. Then she noticed the attachment and clicked on it. After a couple of moments, a photo opened and her heart gave a hard thump in her chest. She didn't know when Angel had taken the photo, but a smiling image of Jason standing next to Brent, who was mounted on a horse, caused an unfamiliar warmth to spread outward from her heart to every part of her body.

Angel's photos always managed to tell a story, and this one showed how much Brent idolized Jason and how the man would do anything to protect the boy. Jason had never said those words, but there was something in his eyes that was more powerful, more expressive, than anything he might have ever said out loud.

Setting aside the caring and kindness, the picture also showcased just how handsome Jason was. If he didn't have women panting after him at every rodeo, it would only be because no women were in attendance. A flicker of jealousy led to her making a frustrated sound at herself. Looking at pictures of Jason wasn't going to make her infatuation go away, and she needed it to go away. Far, far away.

Even knowing that, she couldn't take her eyes off the image of him. The feelings coursing through her were so unlike her, at least the person she'd been once she'd gotten past Blake's abandonment. She'd grown up after that, become someone who didn't need a guy to make her feel important. Not even the ones she'd dated more than once or twice. Of course, there was no way to totally banish the innate need to feel desirable. She'd be lying if she claimed otherwise. Over the years, she'd worked hard to become the person she wanted to be—independent, hardworking, caring—but she couldn't carve out the human need to be wanted and throw it away. She'd admittedly pushed it down whenever it attempted to force its way to the forefront, sometimes taking longer than others, but it never totally went away.

Forcefully pulling herself out of the past, she shut down her laptop and left the room. But even though she was no longer looking at the photo of Jason, the image stuck with her and refused to be dislodged. It took up what felt like permanent residence right next to the memory of how it had felt to be kissed by him.

"Damn it," she said as she stepped into the barn and immediately came to a halt. As she scanned the interior, she wondered if her brain was ever going to operate correctly again.

Because even though she'd left the house and crossed the distance to the barn, she realized she had no idea why.

Chapter Ten

Jason sang along with the song on the radio as he drove down another long Texas road. He didn't want to examine the why too closely, but he'd been in a damn good mood the past few days. Ever since Sloane had texted him congratulations on his win. That talk he'd had with himself about focusing on his work and not on the memory of how she'd felt in his arms didn't have the lasting effect he'd intended. He'd made it through the rodeo successfully, but he hadn't been off his horse five seconds before he'd wished she was there so he could celebrate with her.

Though it was all kinds of crazy, he'd canceled his next event in California and replaced it with yet another rodeo in Texas, near San Antonio, in the hope that he could see her again. He didn't even mind all the extra miles of driving to get back to the Lone Star State. That alone told him he was being irrational.

But irrational felt good at the moment. It would feel even better if Sloane agreed to come see him ride. Of course, he had to ask her first.

He put off the asking until he arrived at the rodeo grounds and unloaded Oscar into the barn and parked his trailer, then again while he checked into his hotel.

He knew it was procrastinating because he liked anticipating seeing her. If he asked and she declined, he was pretty damn sure his mood was going to sour.

Jason sank onto the side of his bed and resisted the sudden need to stretch out. He'd spent the night before at a crappy little motel in a town he was fairly certain wasn't on a road map. A morgue slab had to be more comfortable than the bed he'd attempted to sleep in.

I'm getting too old for this crap.

He refused to put off the call any longer. If she said yes, he wanted to be able to spend as much time with her as possible. Ignoring how nervous he was, he hit her number. After three unanswered rings, the call went to her voice mail.

"Hey, it's Sloane. You missed me, so leave me a message."

The way even her recorded voice caused him to get to his feet and pace was evidence enough that he should be in California right now.

"Sloane, it's Jason. I'm competing down near San Antonio. Thought you might like to swing by."

Swing by? What the hell was he saying? It wasn't as if he was asking her to pop over to the other side of Blue Falls. She could very well be too busy. Might not be interested in seeing him again.

She'd seemed interested enough to kiss him with more than a little heat.

He realized he'd left a long pause in the message. "I've got some extra time, so give me a call if you want to get together."

Before he made himself sound like even more of an idiot, he hung up. That's when he flopped back on the bed and discovered that it was every bit as soft as it looked. As he stared at the ceiling, his lack of sleep and the long hours on the road began to catch up with him.

He closed his eyes, which only gave him a dark backdrop against which to replay their first kiss. His lips stretched into a smile at the memory. He'd kissed a number of women over the years, but none of those kisses had affected him the way Sloane's had and he couldn't articulate why. They just did.

All he knew was his attraction to her had the power to scramble his brain, to make him discard decisions that made sense for ones that made him question his sanity. It was as if the two halves of his brain were in a tug-of-war, one that included a lot of trying to convince himself that spending time with Sloane wouldn't affect his riding. One half pointed out that he'd done poorly the night he'd met her, but the other argued that memories of their kiss had been bouncing around in his head last weekend when he'd won his event. Maybe this weekend would be the tiebreaker.

If she showed up. Which, judging by the silence of the phone still in his hand, didn't seem promising.

Needing rest and not wanting to dwell on the way his phone wasn't ringing, he allowed himself to drift off toward sleep. Maybe Sloane would at least greet him in his dreams.

SLOANE'S HEART WAS still beating fast as she tossed her phone onto the kitchen counter and went back to chopping vegetables for a big pot of soup her mom was making as soon as she got back from town with a couple of ingredients she'd been missing.

"Who was that?" Angel asked as she mixed the batter for a batch of chocolate chip cookies.

"Nobody. Wrong number."

Sloane pulled a couple of carrots from the refrigerator, and when she turned back to the cutting board she spotted Angel with her phone.

"What are you doing?"

"Checking out who nobody was."

Sloane grabbed for the phone, but Angel spun away with a knowing smile on her face. "Funny how 'nobody' is showing up on your phone as one Jason Till, who happens to be programmed into your contacts."

Sloane said nothing in response, knowing anything she said would incriminate her further.

"Why didn't you answer?"

"Why should I?"

"Um, maybe because it was a hot cowboy calling."

"If I want a hot cowboy, I'll just go to the music hall and pick one up."

"No, you won't, because you like Jason."

"Oh, for crying out loud," Sloane said as she started chopping the carrots with guillotine-force slices. "Will you let it go?"

"Sloane, the fact that my teasing is getting to you so much is all the evidence I need to prove that something about Jason stuck with you. That and the fact that your head has been anywhere but here the past week. And he must like you, too, if he's calling you."

"He probably just wants to know if I talked to his sister."

"And the fact that he had his sister contact you in the first place says he isn't just a date-and-disappear kind of guy."

Sloane gestured with the knife. "He rides the rodeo circuit. That's the very definition of *date-and-disappear.*

Damn it, I should have never gone out with him in the first place."

"Of course you should have. You enjoyed it, right? And don't even think about denying it."

"Then why ask me the question?" Sloane had to calm down or she was going to risk chopping off one of her fingers.

"Because you need to admit that you like him, and then you need to do something about it."

"You're as bad as Mom."

"This isn't just me thinking you need to get paired up for the sake of pairing up."

"Then what, pray tell, is it?"

Angel leaned back against the counter and fixed her gaze on Sloane. "I don't want to see you deliberately sabotage something just because you're afraid."

"I'm not afraid. I just have some common sense."

"You are afraid that you'll get hurt the same way you did when Blake left."

Sloane's hand slid on the knife handle and she barely got her vulnerable fingers out of the way in time. "Blake? What's he got to do with anything? That was ages ago."

"And despite how you tried to hide it and refused to talk about the breakup, I could tell he hurt you a lot. And you haven't totally gotten over that."

"I haven't thought about him in forever." At least not until Jason started stirring up all her old feelings of mistrust and abandonment and anger. "And I've dated other people since then."

Not too successfully, but she wasn't about to point that out.

"Sloane, I'm just trying to help you. I know what it's like to be hurt by someone and not want to ever trust someone again, to want to guard your heart. I think what Blake did to you is always there at the back of your mind, even when you're dating someone else, even when you don't realize it. And I totally get that, more than most people."

Sloane set the knife aside and let out a breath. "Then why would you want me to get involved with someone I can't be with?"

"You don't know what the future might hold, but there is something there. It was palpable from the moment you two met, and since he's been gone your brain has been anywhere but in your head."

"I just need more time. Whatever…infatuation there might be will fade."

"Do you really believe that?"

"I have to."

"Why?"

"Because I hate this constant distracted feeling. I need to be able to concentrate on work."

"Maybe your mind is trying to tell you something, that all work and no play makes Sloane—"

"I swear if you say, 'makes Sloane a dull girl…'"

"I was going to say it makes you unhappy and lonely."

"How can I possibly be lonely? I'm surrounded by people who won't leave me in peace."

"It's not the same thing and you know it," Angel said, her tone changing so that she seemed to suddenly sound like the big sister dispensing advice based on personal experience. "Listen to me. I think if you continue to ignore these feelings you have for Jason, you're going to regret it. Sure, he's riding the circuit now and maybe you won't be able to see him all the time, but how often do you go out now anyway? You've been out what, maybe once or twice since you broke up with Jeremy?"

"My dating choices haven't exactly given me a lot of confidence in the male half of the population."

"Understandable, but you know there are good guys out there. As annoying as they can be, our brothers are three of them."

"I know." The begrudging tone of her response would have made her laugh if someone else had said it.

"And you and I both know that no one can ride rodeo forever. Jason is going to have a life after rodeo, and who's to say that life can't be here?"

"You're really getting ahead of yourself now."

"Maybe, maybe not. But I'm telling you what I saw between you two is like nothing I've seen before, and that's coming from someone who sees her besotted brothers every day."

A shiver went through Sloane at the thought that she wanted to believe her sister, wanted to believe there could be something with Jason that wouldn't end up being a huge mistake. The fact that she wanted that so much scared her because she literally didn't feel like herself.

Angel placed her hand atop Sloane's. "You are always doing things for the family, for all those kids who come to the camps. Do something for yourself. Take a chance and call him back." Angel paused for a moment. "Don't let Blake, Jeremy or anyone else steal any more from you."

Her sister's words hit Sloane like a truth bomb. Had she really been letting Blake's long-ago abandonment or Jeremy's betrayal affect her so fundamentally, even when she hadn't been aware of it or consciously thinking about them? That thought ticked her off. The idea that Blake especially still had power over her feelings caused her to grab her phone.

"I'll be back in a minute."

Angel smiled as Sloane passed her on the way to the back door.

Once outside, Sloane's stomach tightened and her entire body felt jittery.

Come on, it's just a phone call.

She took a deep breath and exhaled as she walked across the backyard toward the picnic tables. As she sat atop one of them, she was beginning to think that Jason wasn't going to pick up. But then she heard his voice, and damn if she didn't have the thought that it was a good thing she was sitting down. Why did just the sound of his voice make her feel a little dizzy?

"Hey, how's it going?" he said.

"Good. Busy. You?" *Hello, monosyllabic much?*

"Same. So are you calling to tell me you're going to come see me ride?"

"What?"

"I left you a message that I'm down near San Antonio for a rodeo."

"Oh, I didn't listen to the message. I just saw you called and figured you were checking to see if Shannon contacted me. She did."

"She told me. But no, I'd like to see you."

"I don't know—"

"Did you have fun on our date?"

"Yes, but—"

"Then let's do it again. In fact, I'm free all day tomorrow. I hear they're having a free day at the zoo. I haven't been to a zoo in forever."

The zoo? What were the odds that of all the places in San Antonio, he'd pick that? Was the universe trying to tell her something?

"Don't think too much," he said. "Just come down and have some fun."

"Okay." Had she just agreed to a second date with a man with whom she had no future?

Or was Angel right? Was there a chance, however slight, that there might be some sort of future for her and Jason?

She shook her head. She had to keep those kinds of thoughts from forming. This was just another casual, no-expectations date, two people simply having fun together. If she started thinking about the future and commitment, it would freak her out. She simply wasn't ready for that, might never be. But a bit of fun she could handle.

"Great," he said.

She smiled at the tone of his voice, which sounded as if he was happy with her answer. Or was she reading more into his single-word response than was there? She ran her hand over her face and tried to remember the person she was before Jason strolled into her life and scrambled her brain like a skillet of eggs.

SLOANE SAT IN the zoo's parking lot, debating with herself whether to get out of her truck or head straight back to Blue Falls. She normally didn't experience much confusion about how her days would go, and she liked it that way. But since meeting Jason, she'd felt as if she'd been tossed into a boiling vat of confusion. The rational side of her brain told her that meeting him again was a mistake, that she was just dragging out the inevitable and allowing herself to become more attached, which, of course, would make the eventual end of them that much more unpleasant. But the other part of her brain would not relinquish its grip on him, and she feared that part was growing larger by the day.

Or maybe she was just overthinking every last bit of this potential encounter. If she walked through those zoo gates, she had to do it with her head screwed on right and no expectations.

After taking a deep breath, she opened the door and stepped out into the parking lot.

As she approached the entrance gate, she scanned all the people heading the same direction. Moms pushing strollers and holding the hands of small, excited children. An older couple wearing matching T-shirts that said Retired and Loving It. And then her gaze lit on Jason. She actually stopped and stared at him. He wore faded jeans, boots and a blue T-shirt that made her mouth water so much that barbecue ribs would be jealous. It seemed like some movie special effect, but she'd swear on her life that everything around her screeched into slow motion. Some part of her brain knew she should take a breath, but she found it remarkably difficult. What was happening to her? How could someone she'd only been around a handful of times affect her in such a powerful way?

She watched as he slowly turned his head and spotted her. As he smiled and lifted his hand to wave, the world around her shifted back to normal speed. She nearly tipped over at the sudden motion but headed toward him to cover up her wobbly response to his smile.

"Hey," he said as he met her halfway and gave her a kiss on the cheek that nearly made her moan in pleasure. "Good to see you."

"You, too."

She nervously glanced past him toward the entrance. "So, the zoo, huh? You don't get enough of animals on a daily basis?"

"Not a lot of lions and giraffes on the rodeo circuit." He entwined his fingers with hers and guided her toward the gate.

She wondered if she'd be able to drag her attention away from how great his hand felt around hers enough to notice a single exhibit.

Once they were inside and walking toward the African section, he said, "I wondered if you'd actually come."

"I recall you saying something similar when we met for dinner."

"Well, I felt the same. Nervous as a teenage boy waiting for his first date."

She stopped in the middle of the path, requiring other visitors to choose to go right or left around them. "You were nervous? Why?"

Jason turned to face her. "Because I thought I might not get to do this again."

And then he kissed her right there in the middle of the zoo as if no one else was around. Though some little speck of her brain was aware they were making a scene, the rest didn't care and she kissed him back. Oh, he tasted so good.

Someone whistled, causing her to jerk back to reality. Jason, blast him, just grinned against her lips, then chuckled.

"You're a bad influence," she said as she pushed away.

"Don't stop on our account," a teenage boy walking by with friends called to them.

Heat rushed to Sloane's cheeks. Jason just laughed and escorted her toward the first of the exhibits. They ate ice cream, took goofy photos, fed cups of nectar to the beautiful lorikeets and finally ended up seated on a bench opposite the carousel.

"You look as if you're having a good time," Jason said as he draped his arm around her shoulders.

"I am." More so than she could have even imagined. If only it could last.

Don't think about that now.

"This zoo was the inspiration for my camps."

"You're going to have to help me see the connection," he said.

She stared at the spinning carousel, the large hand-painted animals and the laughing children and was transported back in time.

"I attended an overnight camp here when I was a kid, before I was adopted."

"You lived in San Antonio?"

"Yeah, with my dad. We…" Was she really going to tell a person she barely knew about her past when she didn't even speak of it often with her own family? She glanced over at him and felt her heart expand. She doubted she'd be able to explain what was happening if she were the smartest person in the world, but she found herself wanting to share everything with him, to believe that whatever it was between them wouldn't end as soon as she drove away again. She bit her lip and shifted her gaze back to the carousel. "We were not well-off at all. My mom died when I was so young I don't remember her, but my dad missed her terribly. He did his best to hide it from me. He didn't succeed, but he tried. And then…" A pang of old loss hit her square in the heart.

"He got sick with cancer. Life was really hard, and one of my teachers suggested my dad sign me up for this zoo sleepover. I'd never even been to the zoo because we couldn't afford it, and when I walked through those gates and saw an elephant…it was as if I'd entered another world. I couldn't get enough. Every animal I saw was just amazing, and when we got our meals I ate until I thought my belly would pop." She looked up at the sky. "Sleeping out beneath the stars was something I'll never forget. For that one twenty-four-hour period, I got to live a life that wasn't my own. It didn't have to be hard or sad or filled with worry."

A lump filled her throat, growing larger by the second. "A year later, my dad was gone and I went into foster care. When I was lonely or scared, I'd think about that night at the zoo."

"And you wanted to give that same feeling to other kids in tough situations," Jason said, his voice full of so much understanding that she felt her heart fall for him a bit more despite the heartache that it might eventually cause her.

She nodded. "There are so many kids who either come from impoverished or broken homes, who are bounced around foster care like hot potatoes. I've never told anyone this, but there's a part of me that wishes I could give them all happy, stable homes like my parents did for me and my brothers and sisters. I know that's not possible."

"Maybe not for all of them. I can see you adopting a kid or two though."

He couldn't have surprised her more if he'd said he could picture her as a runway model in Paris.

"I don't know. Helping out kids and being a parent

are two different things. And I've seen how hard it is to be a single parent, so many times. Being a mom or dad is hard enough when there are two people sharing the responsibility."

And the fact that for a moment she could see clearly sharing that type of responsibility with him should tell her more than anything else that she'd made a mistake coming here. She started to stand, but his hand on hers stopped her.

"What do you say we ride that carousel instead of just staring at it?"

His question surprised her, but she latched onto the chance to change the topic of conversation. And when she finished the ride, she'd tell him that it was nice to see him, and then head home.

And stay there, far away from the temptation posed by the man beside her.

Chapter Eleven

Even though it didn't bother him to jump off speeding horses and tackle steers, Jason hated riding things that spun. But he'd sensed that Sloane was about to bolt. She'd honestly surprised him with her confession about her past, and maybe she'd freaked herself out, too. But he liked being with her, perhaps more than liked, and he didn't want her to leave. Honestly, he wanted her to spend the entire weekend with him, but that might be asking too much. As strong and independent as Sloane was, there was also a part of her that was skittish. He'd thought those traits contradictory in the same person, but maybe it had to do with losing her birth parents so young. He couldn't imagine what that must have been like for her. He'd always taken having his parents there when he needed them for granted, even when hundreds of miles separated them.

"Are you sure you want to do this?" Sloane asked, drawing his attention.

"Yeah, why?"

She laughed. "Liar. You look as if all the blood has drained from your face."

"Okay, confession. Me and things that spin don't get along so well. It's why I'm not a bronc or bull rider."

"Then why did you suggest riding the carousel?"

He pulled her around to face him. "Because I didn't want you to leave."

"I didn't say anything about leaving."

"But you were thinking it."

"You're a mind reader now?"

"Didn't need to be to see you were about to race for the exit."

"I wasn't going to race anywhere." She paused. "I would have walked calmly."

"Oh, well, that makes all the difference." He smiled at her and was rewarded with a smile in return.

"What are we doing here?" she asked.

"I thought we were having a good time."

She sighed. "You know what I mean."

"Do I?"

She took a step away from him, breaking contact, and started walking down the path toward the bird exhibit.

"I don't know why I told you all the stuff about my dad and my first trip to this zoo."

"Maybe I'm just one of those people who's easy to talk to."

She glanced over at him. "You are and that's what bothers me."

"Why?"

"You may have noticed I'm not the easiest person to open up, and yet I find myself spilling the beans whenever I'm around you."

He took a chance that she wouldn't jerk away and clasped her hand in his. After a momentary and probably instinctual flinch, her hand relaxed. "And I'm normally someone who moves from town to town with no real attachment to any of the places I visit or the people I meet. Until I met you."

It felt dangerous for him to say that, especially when he knew he might be giving her the wrong impression. Though he'd changed his schedule to come back to the area so he could see her again, he couldn't just compete in Texas the rest of the year and hope to make the Finals.

When he noticed the questioning look she was giving him, he shrugged. "We had a nice time before. Can't blame a guy for wanting a repeat."

That made him sound too much like a player, but instinct told him to dial back the seriousness a bit. For both their sakes.

Part of him didn't want to leave the zoo, but he needed to head to the arena to prepare for that night's opening round of competition. Before they left, she excused herself to the ladies' room. He took the opportunity to duck into the gift shop, all the while not examining too closely why he was buying a gift for Sloane. Oh, who was he kidding? He wanted her to think about him when she looked at it, maybe even decide to stay for the rodeo and possibly for a while afterward.

When he stepped out of the gift shop, he spotted her scanning the area for him. His breath caught in his chest and he found it hard to fill his lungs. With her blond hair up and a few strands escaping the knot atop her head, it struck him just how beautiful she was. More beautiful than he suspected she realized. For a crazy moment, he understood his sister's decision not to pursue rodeo, instead following a different path that included the ultimate commitment to another person.

How could he even be thinking those kinds of thoughts when he'd known Sloane such a short time? Had he given himself some sort of strange concussion that changed his personality?

"Buying something for your niece and nephew?" she asked as she pointed toward the bag he was holding.

"No, you." He extended the bag to her.

"Me? Why?"

"Do I need a reason?"

"Uh, yes."

"Okay. How about I saw how much you liked the giraffes and thought you needed one of your own?"

Sloane's lips parted slightly and she hesitated to accept the bag, as if she thought he might be pulling a joke on her. But then she reached out as if she'd just remembered how to use her arms and took the bag and opened it slowly. The hint of a smile that began to form on her lips made him happier than he'd expected.

"I love it," Sloane said as she pulled out the foot-tall plush animal, then ran her palm along its neck.

Jason wouldn't mind having her hand skim along his body the same way.

She looked up at him as she held the giraffe close. "That night I spent here as a kid, I slept across from the giraffe enclosure. They've always been my favorite animal."

"I'm glad you like it."

They stared at each other for what seemed like much longer than the few seconds it probably was, and Jason felt something shift inside him. Something he hadn't even known was there. Something he couldn't name or explain.

"I guess you should be getting to work, huh?"

Sloane's question jolted him away from his wandering thoughts.

"Uh, yeah. Will you come to the rodeo?"

She hesitated for a moment, during which he felt himself holding his breath, but then smiled.

"I'm already in the area, so I might as well."

He smiled, happy to know she'd be there watching as he tried to take another step toward his ultimate goal. Now all he had to do was make sure he didn't have a repeat of the first night of the Blue Falls Rodeo when thoughts of her had caused him to put his path to the Finals in jeopardy.

SLOANE WATCHED JASON position his horse in the box. She bit her lip and gripped the edge of the bleacher where she was seated. She didn't think she'd ever been so nervous watching something that didn't affect her at all. But her day with Jason had been great, even if it had spooked her how easily she could imagine allowing herself to fall for him. Others might find it ridiculous how much that little stuffed giraffe had touched her, but it had. It couldn't have meant more if he'd bought an entire ranch for her. He deserved to do well tonight not only because he worked hard but also because all the evidence so far told her he was a good guy.

She inhaled sharply when he gave the quick nod that led to the release of the steer. She doubted her heart managed to beat three times before he leaped off his galloping horse and tackled the steer. And when he got all four of its feet off the ground and the official waved his flag, the clock showed he had the fastest time of the night. Sloane jumped to her feet and cheered with so much enthusiasm that she drew a few stares from other spectators. She didn't care.

It hit her how nice it was to be able to show how

she really felt without worrying about what everyone around her—people she worked with on the camps, her family, basically everyone in Blue Falls—thought. There were no expectations or hopes from strangers, and she took a long, deep breath of that freedom before sitting back down with a big smile on her face.

Nervousness knotted in her stomach until the rides of the last two steer wrestlers were over and she was sure Jason had won the night. She looked toward the end of the arena and spotted him looking right at her. She'd swear she felt the force of his gaze as if it were a physical touch.

She broke eye contact in order to draw breath, something she'd somehow not been able to do while her gaze was locked with his. Suddenly unable to sit still, she took the stairs down to the ground and headed for the concession stand. When she turned away from paying for a giant Coke and an order of nachos a few minutes later, she came face-to-face with the man who made her heart race faster than any horse on the premises.

"I would have taken you to dinner afterward, you know."

She lifted the nachos. "I doubt it would be better than nachos."

He smiled. "Willing to share?"

"Hell, no. Get your own, cowboy."

Jason laughed and made an exaggerated bow to her as he backed his way into the line. She rolled her eyes and stood off to the side, eating her nachos with a lot of slow-motion relish.

"You're evil," Jason called to her.

She responded by sucking a dollop of nacho cheese off her finger. The look on Jason's face changed from

teasing to something very different. It hit her that her
action might have looked provocative, even if that
hadn't been her intent. She had so little experience trying to be seductive and was pretty sure she'd look like
an idiot if she tried.

Or maybe not. For a moment, she thought Jason
might march right out of line toward her. She'd swear
she saw him lick his lips before he turned his attention
forward toward the concession stand.

She took the opportunity to walk away. While the
commonsense part of her brain told her to take her nachos and head for the parking lot, she instead retraced
her steps to the grandstand. To try to keep her mind off
what had just passed silently between her and Jason, she
shoved nachos in her mouth as she watched the activity
in the arena, only vaguely aware it was team roping.

She sensed Jason's presence before she saw him at
the bottom of the concrete steps. He hesitated for a moment before climbing toward her. She'd swear under
oath that her heartbeat increased twofold with each step
he took.

"What'd I miss?" he asked as he sat beside her.

She almost exhaled in relief so loudly he and half
the grandstand's occupants could have heard her. "Not
much. I honestly was more focused on these nachos."

"We should have eaten more at the zoo."

But there she'd been too busy divulging her past and
enjoying the feel of Jason's hand around hers.

She didn't know whether he sensed her nervousness
or wanted to pretend the charged moment between them
hadn't happened, but Jason steered the conversation in
safe directions as they watched the rodeo events.

"So, after talking to Shannon, do you think you

can use any of the ideas she gave you to help fund the camps?" he asked.

"I hope so. I floated an idea I'd seen elsewhere to see what she thought. Even though it sounds completely crazy that anyone would buy so-called artwork done by animals, she said it's amazing what philanthropists will buy. I guess if elephants do it, why not cows and horses?"

He shook his head. "Maybe I should splash some paint on a canvas and you can sell it as art by an honest-to-goodness rodeo cowboy?"

She laughed at that. "Now, that might be stretching it too far."

"You're probably right."

"But speaking of rodeo cowboys, what do you think your chances are of making the National Finals?"

"I don't even want to hazard a guess. There are a lot of moving parts that have to land in my favor each and every week." He looked over at her and smiled that dead-sexy smile of his. "But it seems you were my lucky charm tonight. Maybe I should take you to every rodeo."

"Well, that would be difficult since I have my own life to live. You're lucky I showed up today."

"Yeah, I am."

The way his voice rumbled and the intensity of his gaze on her made every square inch of her flesh tingle. She knew she should look away, focus on the barrel racing currently going on, but she couldn't.

"You have a burning need to watch bull riding, or would you like to leave a little early?"

"Early." Okay, her response was way too breathy, revealed way too much of how she yearned for Jason's hands on her more with each passing second.

He evidently needed no further permission because

he grasped her hand and headed for the stairs. By no means were her legs short, but even she was breathless by the time they reached the semidarkness of the parking lot. She suspected that had less to do with the speed of their departure and more with what awaited them at the end of the journey.

An arrow of common sense pierced her haze of lust, screaming that she needed to halt this before it went too far.

"Jason, I—"

Before she could finish saying whatever it was she'd been about to say, Jason turned and pulled her into his arms. His mouth met hers in a kiss that brought to mind molten chocolate and a bed full of tangled sheets. He deepened the kiss as his arms came around her, and she let go of every reason this was the king of bad ideas.

She was only vaguely aware that they sometimes came up for air, but other than that there was no room in her head beyond the processing of all the delicious sensations running across her skin, along every synapse in her brain and straight to…well, other places. She hadn't felt this out of control since—

Sloane pulled away from Jason so suddenly she almost catapulted herself back onto her butt. Of all the times for Blake's stupid face to invade her memories.

But maybe that was actually for the best. Something needed to remind her that while she loved spending time with Jason, he was temporary, would be gone yet again in a couple of days. Someday he'd be as permanently gone as Blake was, and she had no intention of allowing her heart to go through the same kind of trauma that it had all those years ago.

"Are you okay?" Jason said as he started to reach for her.

She waved off his concern. "Yeah, fine. I just…need to be getting home. Mom worries if we're out too late."

Said the twenty-nine-year-old woman. She barely prevented herself from a huge eye roll at herself, but she couldn't take back the excuse now. And to make matters worse, Jason appeared to doubt her reasoning.

"I had a nice time today though," she said.

"Me, too." He eased forward and this time she didn't jump like a scared bunny. "Though I'll admit I was hoping you'd stay awhile longer."

He had no idea how much she wanted to do exactly that. But doing so went against every scrap of common sense she still possessed.

"Jason, I—"

"I understand. I'm disappointed, but I understand."

He couldn't possibly, but she wasn't about to delve into another part of her past, the part that had been the result of the biggest mistake of her life.

Jason gently cupped her face and kissed her, sweet and tender this time. "Come back tomorrow?"

"I don't know," she said against his lips.

"That's better than a flat-out no. I'll have to convince you with my charm."

She smiled at that. "You sound awfully confident you possess charm."

"I am the guy who got you a stuffed giraffe."

"Details, details."

His smile weakened her resolve considerably, almost to the point where she asked him to lead her to the nearest hotel room. Marshaling her dwindling brain cells, she once again put distance between them.

"If I don't see you tomorrow, good luck with the rest of the competition."

He gave her a mischievous grin. "I'll get you back here."

There was a more than fair chance he was right. She laughed a little before heading toward where she'd parked. At least she thought she was going the right direction. As filled as her head was of thoughts of Jason and how a large part of her wanted to strip him naked, it was possible she'd walk the entire parking area and still not notice her truck.

JASON WATCHED SLOANE walk away, wondering despite his bravado if it would be the last time he saw her. She obviously had more sense than he did, ending the evening before things went any further. But damn, he wanted to go after her. He might not have known her long, but it felt like much longer, as if each minute equated to a month in real time. And he really, really liked her, more than was wise considering their lives were so different, being led miles apart. States apart.

And though Sloane didn't seem like the type of woman on the hunt for a husband, he also somehow knew she wasn't the type to sleep around casually either. Which left him with letting her go and hoping the intense attraction went away before one of them totally ditched their chosen path. He knew how much her family and the camps meant to her, way more than a guy who might offer a fun diversion but nothing else. Plus his big goal and sticking around central Texas weren't compatible. Half of him still couldn't believe he'd changed his schedule and driven all the extra miles just for the possibility of seeing her again. It hadn't even been a guarantee.

His phone rang, and in the couple of moments he looked away from Sloane to reach for the phone she disappeared from sight. He ignored the disappointment that made an appearance and answered the call from his dad.

"So, how'd it go? Your decision to switch events pay off?" his dad asked.

"Good first night. Had the fastest time."

"That's my boy. I tell you, this is the year. You're going all the way."

That was the plan, but Jason couldn't help the twist of anxiety at the expectations his parents had placed on him, especially his father. He couldn't blame his dad for living vicariously, especially when his own career had been cut short. Jason would never admit it out loud, but he wished there wasn't so much riding on each and every performance. Not that he wouldn't put pressure on himself to win, but having other people's hopes and dreams pinned on how well he did could sometimes feel like a weight was crushing him little by little.

Why had that thought bubbled to the top? Most of the time he just accepted his parents' expectations as a point of fact and moved on.

Maybe it was because his brain was already scrambled by a certain beautiful blonde.

"That's the plan," he said, then proceeded to ask the usual array of questions as he made his way back toward the far side of the barn where he'd parked his truck. Halfway there, his mom picked up the other extension.

"Shannon tells me you met a woman."

What was up with that curious tone to his mother's

voice? It sounded suspiciously like a matchmaking mama, something his mom had never been.

"You're going to have to be more specific. I meet lots of women." Okay, that didn't come out right.

"The one who runs the camps. She sounds like a lovely person, doing that for kids who are less fortunate."

"It's a good program. The kids really like it."

"Anything else there?"

He had to get her off this topic. "Who are you, and what have you done with my mother?"

"Jane, leave the boy alone," his dad said, gently scolding. "He's got more important things he needs to focus on."

"Fine," his mom said in response, sounding a touch exasperated. "Good luck tomorrow night, hon."

"Thanks, Mom."

After the conversation with his dad ended and Jason was on his way back to his hotel room, one he had to admit he had imagined sharing with Sloane, the easy way his dad had dismissed the idea of him finding someone didn't quite sit right for some reason. Not that he'd given his parents any indication he might be looking for a relationship. Hell, he couldn't remember the last time he'd even thought about it himself. And it made next to no sense that the thought was bouncing around in his head now.

It had to be a case of inflated infatuation, though why it was hitting him now and with this woman in particular he didn't know. As he'd told his mom, he met plenty of women. Beautiful, funny women. Some were also smart and successful. Others showed their caring natures in various ways.

But Sloane was all those things inhabiting one body, and he'd been drawn to her at first sight.

When he reached his room, he pulled out his computer and did what he usually did—checked the latest news from around the circuit, scanned the standings, examined the options for upcoming rodeos. Texas was a big state, one full of rodeos. Maybe he wouldn't have to go far for his next competition, could convince Sloane to agree to another date. He still fully intended to persuade her to see him the next day, but there wasn't anything wrong with looking ahead.

But as he perused the standings and upcoming rodeos, he realized he could hang around Texas in order to spend time with Sloane or he could stick to the schedule he'd outlined that would give him the best chance to make the Finals, but not both. His dad really believed Jason was going to get back to the Finals this year, and Jason didn't want to disappoint him. This might be the last chance their family got for some rodeo glory. And the paycheck and potential endorsement deals that came with it.

A heavy, tired feeling settled in his chest, so he shut the computer and went to the bathroom to take a shower. When he stepped under the flow of water, he realized that thoughts of Sloane had followed him. Those thoughts transformed to hot and steamy daydreams about having her in the shower with him. He ran his hand over his face. He suspected this would be what Shannon called "having it bad."

He made quick work of the shower, hoping his thoughts of Sloane would fade enough that he'd be able to sleep. Right now, sleep was the furthest thing from his mind.

He flopped down on the bed and grabbed his phone.

It wouldn't hurt to text Sloane to make sure she'd made it home safely. That's what any decent guy would do.

Of course, the images he'd had of her over the past several minutes couldn't be described as decent.

He cursed at himself as he typed and sent off a quick message. If he had a lick of sense, he'd set the phone aside and try to get some sleep. Instead, he stared at the small screen, waiting for a response to appear.

Chapter Twelve

Sloane was pretty sure her heart continued to race all the way back to Blue Falls. At this rate, she was going to have to drive straight to the ER to get something to slow it down. But the way Jason kissed her kept playing on repeat in her head, sending shivers of need dancing across her body. She felt as if someone else's personality was invading and supplanting hers. She wasn't this person who wanted to spend an entire weekend in bed with a guy she didn't know anywhere near well enough. And that's exactly what she'd wanted before she'd barely pulled herself away from Jason and left him standing in that parking lot.

She had to stay away from him. No way was she going back to see him ride the next night. Twice she'd gone out with him, and twice it'd felt as if she was losing control to a wildfire.

As she pulled into the ranch a few minutes later, she realized that her head had been so thoroughly filled with Jason that she hadn't thought about how to explain where she'd been all day and evening. She didn't want to lie, but telling the truth was almost as unappealing. Especially if her mom was within hearing range. Sloane parked and sat staring out the windshield at the darkness that lay beyond.

She realized that the longer she sat out here, the more curious anyone waiting inside was going to be, and yet she couldn't make herself move. Even though she'd thought about Jason all the way back home, she wanted to indulge just a bit longer before she had to go inside and pretend nothing earth-shattering had happened.

With her eyes closed, she let her mind replay the entire day, from when she'd spotted him at the zoo entrance until he'd pulled her into his arms like some romantic hero in a movie.

A knock on the driver's-side window made her jerk and yelp as if she'd opened her bedroom closet to find a chain saw–wielding clown waiting for her. She clasped her chest in a vain effort to calm the explosion of her heart's beating. It took a few of those thundering beats for her to realize the person on the other side of the glass was Ben. And he was wearing a big ol' grin.

Sloane opened her door so fast she nearly slammed it into her brother. He would deserve it.

"Are you trying to give me a heart attack?"

He chuckled in response, which irritated her even more.

"Seriously, what the hell?"

"I figured I deserved a little bit of fun for saving you."

"What on earth are you talking about?"

He pointed toward the house. "Mom figured out where you were."

Sloane glanced toward the house. "How did… Wait, how did you figure it out?" She knew there was no sense denying the truth. If she did, it would make her day with Jason seem more important than it was, and he'd tease her unmercifully. Probably still would, but it was a matter of degrees at this point.

"She asked Angel where you and Jason were going for your date."

"Angel spilled?"

"Not on purpose. The way Mom asked the question, it was designed to catch Angel off guard and it worked. She didn't have to say anything. The look on her face confirmed what Mom suspected."

Sloane cursed and took a few steps along the side of her truck before gripping the side of the bed with both hands.

"It was only a matter of time," Ben said as he came to stand beside her. "The woman is psychic or something. And it's not exactly like you to go off without explanation."

"I blame you and Neil for this. You put the idea of weddings and babies in her head. Now she sees every casual date as a potential happily-ever-after."

"Is it?"

She looked at her brother as if he'd fallen victim to body snatchers. "Of course not. Kind of hard to have happily-ever-after when one of the people isn't even around."

"True, but sometimes they come back. Look at Arden."

Neil's wife had tried to go back to her job as an international reporter overseas after he'd helped her heal from the trauma of being held captive by human traffickers. But she'd barely landed in Europe when she'd realized she missed and loved Neil more than her old career. She was still a journalist, a good one, but she was forging a new path that allowed her to be with the man she loved.

"That's different."

"How?"

"It just is."

Ben laughed again. "Great comeback."

"Oh, shut up."

They stood in silence for a few moments before Ben spoke again. "Did I ever tell you about the time Neil and I ran into Blake Sharpe up in Fort Worth and I damn near broke his nose?"

Sloane stiffened at the mention of her ex-boyfriend's name. "No, and why are you bringing it up now?"

He shrugged. "Just thought you might like to know."

Ben didn't have to explain further, but what he'd done touched her. She'd evidently not been as good at hiding her pain when Blake had left her as she'd believed. And that made her angry at him all over again.

Ben walked away before she could think of an appropriate response. Even though she'd never been one to need her brothers to fight her battles for her, she had to admit she liked the idea that Blake had earned himself a bit of Hartley retribution. She might have punched him herself if she'd been there. She wasn't the same heartbroken girl she'd been when Blake had dumped her at the worst possible moment.

She wasn't sure what Ben hoped she'd glean from the story about the punishment of Blake's nose, but she took the reminder of what Blake had done as a sign that she was allowing herself to get too caught up in a guy again. She'd sworn to herself she'd never repeat that mistake, which probably explained why Jeremy's hookup with the barrel racer hadn't crushed her more. It had sucked, but not crush-her-heart-to-bits suck.

She took a few more minutes to get her emotions under control and envision how she'd respond when she went inside. Remembering her plush giraffe, she opened the truck's door and retrieved the toy. Unable to keep herself from doing so, she smiled. It really had been a great day and she'd honestly like a repeat. Several repeats. But sometimes you just didn't get what you wanted because it wasn't in the cards.

Without even thinking, she hugged the giraffe close. Warmth spread throughout her body, but the strongest concentration was around her heart. For a moment, she allowed herself to wish Jason lived nearby, that maybe she could finally believe she could try loving someone again.

She startled at that last thought. Love? She wasn't anywhere near loving Jason. She didn't know him well enough. He might have some annoying habit that had yet to reveal itself that would totally turn her off. Or he could really be a jerk and was just hiding it well.

Of course, she wasn't ever going to find out any of those things, especially not anything approaching love.

But why had the word effortlessly made its way into her thoughts in the first place?

Didn't matter. Wasn't happening.

Figuring she might as well get the impending gauntlet over with, she headed for the house. When she stepped through the front door, the bright look of hope on her mom's face was so comical that Sloane almost laughed.

"You look as if you won the lottery, the county fair cake bake-off and were given a new puppy all on the same day."

"I hear you had a date with Jason."

"You didn't hear. You wheedled it out of Angel."

Her mom looked momentarily surprised, then scrunched up her lips. "Ben has a big mouth."

"He had the decency to tell me I was about to be ambushed."

"Ambushed? Well, that's a bit dramatic."

Sloane faced her mom head-on. "Yes, I saw Jason, but you need to let go of the fantasy that we're going to be riding off into some romantic sunset together. We went to the zoo, then a rodeo. We had fun, the end."

"I'm not so sure about that."

"Believe what you want, Mom. Won't change reality."

"Don't you think you're protesting the idea too much?" Her mom lifted an eyebrow in a way that said she believed she'd won the argument.

"Nope." Sloane headed toward her bedroom.

"Sloane."

She halted and looked back at her mom.

"I just want you to be happy, and whether you want to admit it or not, that boy makes you happy."

"So does chocolate cake."

Her mom sighed. "I thought Ben was stubborn."

Sloane just grinned and made for her room. The door had barely closed behind her when her phone dinged with a text message. Her immediate response was a fluttering of her pulse even before she looked at the display and saw it was from Jason. She glanced back at the door as if her mom might burst in and say, "I told you so!"

She shook her head and read his message.

Call me cheesy, but just checking if you got home OK.

She sank onto the edge of her bed and smiled at his thoughtfulness. Granted, he might just be trying to get her to come back for day two of his rodeo so they could pick up where they left off, but it made her happy anyway. Stupidly happy.

She flopped back on the bed and stared at the ceiling. The truth was she did want to go back and not run off next time. But she suspected that while it might be awesome as it was happening, she'd kick herself for being an idiot after the fact. Maybe sooner rather than later.

Considering he couldn't see or hear her, wasn't even in the same county, it was silly how fast her heart was thumping as she began to text a reply.

Yep, fine. Hitting the hay.

Hope your bed is more comfortable than mine was the other night. When I retire, maybe I'll write a guide to the country's worst motels.

She smiled wide at that image, him in his cowboy attire pecking away at a computer. Though his author picture on the dust jacket would certainly be attractive.

She reread the message a couple of times, trying to decide how to respond. Or whether she should respond at all. Maybe she could just pretend that she'd gone to sleep, which was plausible since she'd told him she was hitting the hay. But despite her protestations that there was nothing really between them and the fact that she'd darn near run away from him, she didn't want the night to end.

I'm sure it would be a bestseller.

Ha. I'd only sell copies to buckle bunnies wanting to know where all the rodeo cowboys stay.

Sloane's jaw tightened at the idea of a buckle bunny showing up at Jason's door tonight. Would he let the woman in? After all, she'd in effect declined his implied invitation. She should let the comment go without responding, but she found herself typing back with more force on her screen than was necessary.

I don't understand those women. No self-esteem.

They seem to think pretty highly of themselves.

Her eyes narrowed as she wondered just how many women Jason had slept with and left after one night. She'd been right to leave when she did. And yet she couldn't seem to toss her phone aside and go to bed.

That right?

He didn't immediately respond, and she couldn't help the image of some overly made-up fake cowgirl standing in his open motel room doorway. Or maybe he'd somehow read her accusatory tone and decided that was enough texting with the crazy lady.

Are you jealous?

No. Okay, she'd typed that too quickly, probably negating the answer. Because as daft as it was, the idea of him with someone else did make her jealous. Growling, push-someone-in-the-lake jealous. Ugh, she didn't want to be that person.

A smiley face appeared on her screen. She imagined him grinning ear to ear somewhere in a dumpy motel room. She was about to turn off her phone when another text arrived.

I'm not interested in them. I'm interested in you.

Her breath caught, and her heart started doing that racing thing again. It was scary how much his admission filled her with a warm, giddy feeling.

You're a nice guy. I have fun with you. But we both know this isn't going anywhere.

She paused a moment before typing a bit more. I can't see you anymore.

Unexpectedly, tears formed in her eyes and she had to blink several times to keep them at bay. It became increasingly hard to do as she stared at her phone and the lack of response from his end. But what was he supposed to say? She'd basically just told him to buzz off because he couldn't commit. How could she expect him to commit when they barely knew each other? When it made absolutely no sense that at least some part of her wanted that commitment?

Her heart leaped when the phone finally dinged again.

Have a good night, Sloane.

And just like that her heart sank all the way to her

feet. Her hands actually shook as she typed, You, too. And good luck tomorrow night.

Thanks.

She waited way too long to see if he sent any more messages. But none came.

She'd finally made sure what she'd told her mother was true. There was nothing between her and Jason. It was for the best, but the painfully heavy feeling in her chest told her it wasn't what she wanted.

JASON HAD BEEN in a piss-poor mood all day, a complete one-eighty from the previous day. Even the texting with Sloane the night before had been fun—right up until she'd basically said she never wanted to see him again. He'd known she had walls but had thought he'd been finding his way past them. Evidently they'd gone back up with lightning speed somewhere in the midst of their text conversation.

Maybe she was right. Who knew when he'd be back in Texas again? His father's words came back to him, that Jason had more important things to worry about than a woman. He tried focusing on that night's ride, another step toward the ultimate goal. But his stupid brain kept veering off in the direction of Sloane Hartley. Damn, he needed to get that woman out of his head.

He took the large iced tea he'd brought back from the diner where he'd eaten a late breakfast and plunked down in a chair beside the sad little pool at his motel. No one else was around, and he couldn't blame them. Despite having decent beds, the place was depressing. He took off his boots, rolled up his jeans to his knees and moved to the edge of the pool. Dangling his feet in the water, he took a big swig of his tea.

When his phone started ringing, he grabbed it so quickly he nearly fumbled it into the water. Thank goodness no one was around to see that feat of grace.

He tried not to think about how happy he was that Sloane was calling him. Maybe she'd changed her mind and was coming back today. Having her here would certainly improve the scenery.

But when he looked at the phone, he saw the name on the display wasn't Sloane, but rather his sister. He told himself he was a fool before answering.

"Hey, sis," he said.

"Hey, yourself. Mom just told me you did well last night."

"Can't complain." At least not about the rodeo part of the evening.

"Got a quick question. I talked to your friend Sloane a few days ago, and I was wondering if she'd said anything to you about the ideas we discussed. I was curious if she's going to implement any of them."

Ignoring the extra bit of emphasis Shannon put on *your friend*, he asked, "Why don't you ask her?"

"Well, she and I don't know each other, and I don't want it to seem like I'm pressuring her just because I gave her a bit of advice."

"I haven't talked to her much, but she mentioned that you'd given her some suggestions. I'm sure she appreciates it."

"Okay, what's wrong? You sound like Old Man Farragut."

Great, he sounded like the surliest old fart in the southern half of Idaho.

"Is this about Sloane? You like her, don't you?"

"How could you possibly know that?"

"So you do. What's the problem?"

In that moment, he wanted to toss his phone into the pool—deliberately this time. "Not sure."

"Tell me everything."

"I do not need dating advice from my sister."

"Sure you do. I think we both know that."

He snorted but he also didn't hang up. Instead, he surprised himself by doing as she'd commanded—telling her everything. He didn't realize how long he'd gone on until he detailed the last of the texts he and Sloane had exchanged the night before and finally stopped talking.

"My diagnosis, you're seriously falling for her."

"How is that even possible? I barely know her."

"Quality beats quantity in the world of love."

"That sounds like some cheesy slogan." He sloshed one of his feet forward and took another drink of his tea, only to discover the ice had melted so much that it tasted watered down. Figured.

"Be that as it may, what are you going to do about it?"

"Didn't you hear the part where she said she couldn't see me anymore?"

"My instinct is there is more to the story. If she had a nice time during your dates like you said, then something happened that either changed the situation or scared her."

"She doesn't strike me as the type to scare easily." Although she had beat a hasty retreat the night before when their kissing had gotten hot and heavy.

"The people who appear the strongest are often the best at hiding something they fear makes them weak."

"Are you in marketing or are you a shrink?"

"Both have to be good at reading people and figuring out how they think."

He considered her words for a few moments. "It doesn't really make sense to push this. I mean, we don't live in the same state. And her life is here. Mine's on the road most of the time."

"People have made relationships work under way more difficult circumstances."

"Maybe she doesn't even want a relationship."

"You won't know until you ask."

"She put an end to things. If I press, doesn't that make me a stalker?"

"Now you're just making up excuses because you're scared that this is something real."

"I'm not scared."

"Don't argue with your big sister. Listen, I'm a woman, so I know how women think. You don't have to come across all stalkery to make your feelings known. Now, you know her better than I do, so figure out how you can let her know that you don't want things to end, something that is personal instead of the universal flowers and chocolates."

"I thought all women liked flowers and chocolates." Although Sloane hadn't seemed overly thrilled the first time he brought her flowers.

"At the right time, yes. But it's also too common for a big 'give us a chance' gesture."

"Then what?"

"That, little brother, you have to figure out."

For the rest of the afternoon, he came up with and discarded one idea after another. Nothing felt right. When it came time to head to the rodeo grounds, he gave up. Maybe something would come to him later when he wasn't thinking about it so hard.

Or maybe Shannon was wrong and he needed to just leave things alone, let Sloane live her life and continue to live his. The life that required him to get his head in the game and win this dang rodeo.

Chapter Thirteen

"That's it, boy," Sloane said as she guided her horse through the blue paint and then onto the large sheet of paper. "You'll be the Picasso of the equine world."

"How's it going?" her mom asked as she came into the barn.

"About as well as can be expected. I just hope I'm not laughed out of the country with this." She gestured to where she had several art pieces courtesy of horses and cows hanging from the stalls to dry.

"I doubt anyone is going to laugh at a good cause. In fact, I have some good news for you."

"Oh, yeah?" She could use some positive news to cheer her up. She'd done her best to hide it, but she'd been miserable during the three days since she'd left Jason standing in that parking lot at the rodeo. She'd done the right thing, but it sure had made her feel like a twisted-up mess of angry and sad. She had half a mind to look up Blake and go give him a second dose of busted nose for how he'd contributed to her trust issues. Maybe Jeremy, too. As if losing both of her parents and being ripped from the only home she'd ever known as a young child hadn't been enough.

"I just got off the phone with Merline Teague. She

wants to have an exhibit at the gallery of the paintings, complete with an opening night party and some press."

Sloane stared at her mom as if she was speaking Portuguese. "They're hoofprints. I already feel embarrassed that I'm going to ask money for these."

"Have you seen some of the stuff that brings big dollars in the art world? I swear some of it looks as if it was done by infants." She gestured toward the drying paintings around the barn. "These are every bit as good, if not better."

Sloane scanned what she'd spent the entire morning working on. "Maybe you're right."

"Don't say that as if you're so surprised. I'm right more than my children like to give me credit for." She said it in a teasing way, but Sloane suspected her mom was talking about Jason as much or more than she was the equine and bovine paintings.

The sound of an approaching vehicle drew their attention.

"I'll check to see who that is," her mom said, then headed back outside.

Sloane was in the midst of cleaning the paint off the horse's shoe when a woman appeared at the entrance to the barn. It took her a minute to realize it was Rosita from the food truck in Poppy. What in the world was she doing here?

"Hello. Can I help you?"

Rosita held up a box. "I have a delivery for you."

Sloane tilted her head slightly. "I didn't order anything. And I didn't know you delivered."

Rosita smiled and walked forward. "Special delivery."

Curiosity piqued, Sloane accepted the box.

"Hope you enjoy," Rosita said with a big smile that

seemed to say she was privy to a secret, then she retraced her steps out of the barn.

This day was getting stranger by the minute.

Sloane sank down onto a stack of hay bales and opened the box to find half a dozen of Rosita's famous sopaipillas. Her mouth watered in response. She spotted an envelope at the side of the box and got a funny, fluttery feeling in her stomach.

She tried to ignore how much she wanted this surprise to be from Jason as she opened the envelope. Inside was a card.

I know you said you couldn't see me anymore, but I don't like that idea. I'm hoping I can bribe you with sopaipillas. A pretty girl once told me these were the best ones around. I'm going to be competing in Dallas next weekend. I hope you'll come up. I'm including tickets. Also, you'll find a check in here, and no, it's not bribery. I want you to use it for the camps, however you see fit. I want you to be able to help more kids—for their sake and yours. Hope to see you soon,
Jason

She reread the note, slower this time so she could savor every word as if they were bites of decadent chocolate. He wasn't playing fair. How could she say no after such a thoughtful gesture? Maybe she could see him whenever the chance presented itself if she didn't allow her feelings for him to deepen any further. She couldn't think about how, with this special delivery, she was dangerously close to falling head over heels, crazy as that might seem.

SLOANE HADN'T FULLY anticipated how nervous she'd be when she was on the verge of seeing Jason again. At least half a dozen times between Blue Falls and Dallas, she'd almost turned around. But if she did, she'd have to explain to her entire family why she'd chickened out. There'd been no hiding the reason for this trip from them. She'd taken the teasing and been grateful for how much her mom held her absolute glee in check. It was no use trying to tell any of them that whatever was between her and Jason wasn't so serious that they should get used to seeing him around. Even though she knew his life was still on the road, she hadn't been able to deny herself what she'd been yearning for since the moment she'd met the blasted man.

When she arrived at the indoor arena, she debated whether she should go find him or wait until he'd competed. She didn't want to distract him when he needed to focus on riding well and staying safe. The more she got to know him, the more nervous watching him ride made her. Who in their right mind jumped off a racing horse to land on a horned animal? No one, that's who.

Deciding to put off facing him awhile longer, she bought a soda and a hot pretzel from the concession stand and found a seat with a good view of the dirt-covered arena floor. During the bareback riding, she kept scanning the arena trying to find Jason. Though she'd attended more rodeos in her life than she could count, it really hit her just how many cowboys were in attendance. From a distance, they all looked remarkably similar below their hats.

But as the steer wrestlers gathered behind the pens, she thought she spotted him. Her breath caught and her heart pounded against her ribs. The first two competitors made their runs before she was certain she saw him astride his horse. It was a good thing her mom wasn't around because Sloane felt her mouth spread into a wide grin that no doubt telegraphed all of her feelings.

She watched, barely breathing, as he and his hazer got into position.

Please let him do well and stay safe.

When he gave the slight nod to indicate he was ready and the steer was released, her heart leaped.

"Go, Jason!"

It all happened so fast. One minute he was in the saddle, and the next he was leaning off the side of his racing horse. A surge of fear went through her as he grabbed hold of the steer's horns. Only once he'd flipped the steer onto its side and jumped to his feet with his arms in the air did she draw another breath. She didn't even hear the time, but by the crowd reaction it must have been good. She cheered along with all those around her, but she kept her eyes on Jason as he made his way toward the end of the arena.

Unable to sit still any longer, she jumped up and hurried down the bleachers. She knew she couldn't go back behind the stock pens, but she had to at least pace off some of her nervous energy.

"Sloane."

She stopped at the end of the bleachers, looked toward the sound of her name and made eye contact with Jason. Time went wonky, bending into new shapes as they stared at each other. Then slowly a grin formed on his lips and he stalked toward her. Without a word, he took her hand and led her outside, around the building and into a patch of darkness. Then, much as he had in that parking lot outside San Antonio, he spun her into his arms and kissed her so deeply she felt heat spiral throughout every inch of her body.

Sloane gripped his biceps, then let her hands slide over his shoulders and up his neck into his hair, knocking off his hat.

"Please tell me you're not going home tonight," he said against her lips.

"I'm not going home tonight."

After another round of enthusiastic kissing, complete with a lot of roaming hands, he grasped her hand again and started walking toward the parking lot. She didn't even pretend not to know where they were going. For this one night, she was going to indulge every fantasy she'd had about him since first looking up to see who owned the deep, friendly voice beside the arena in Blue Falls.

When they reached his truck, he ran his fingertips along her jaw. "I want you to spend the night with me, but I don't want to pressure you."

"You're not," she said, leaving no doubt she wanted exactly what he did.

After giving her a quick kiss and helping her into the truck, he ran to his side and exceeded the speed limit the few miles to his hotel. Thankfully, tonight he was staying in a place that probably wouldn't make his book about crappy motels.

"I took a chance you'd be here tonight and decided to take my hotel game up a notch." His grin made her laugh, but in her mind she was already imagining going to bed with him.

"Are you hungry?" he asked as they sat in the lot outside the hotel.

"Food can wait."

She'd swear she saw flames of desire flash in his eyes at her answer.

"I couldn't agree more," he said before practically leaping out of the truck and sprinting around to her side by the time she got the door open.

He appeared to be as nervous as she was because he fumbled and dropped his magnetic keycard to gain access through a side entrance. She couldn't help but chuckle at how he cursed his clumsiness.

"Laugh now, but I won't be this uncoordinated when we get inside."

If he kept talking like that, her skin was going to catch on fire before they ever made it to his room.

They were walking so fast they nearly crashed into an older guy who came around the corner holding a couple of cans of soda, a bag of corn chips and a package of mini powdered doughnuts.

"Sorry," Jason said.

The older man just grinned, as if he'd read their minds. "Don't mind me. I was young once."

Heat suffused Sloane's face, but Jason just laughed a little as they headed in the opposite direction. When Jason finally stopped in front of a room, he glanced over at her.

"Your face is red."

"I feel weird knowing that some old guy eating corn chips knows what we're doing."

Jason grinned. "And what are we doing?"

She lifted a brow. "About to watch nature documentaries, of course."

He pushed open the door and led her inside. "That TV isn't even going to get turned on, but I'm hoping you are."

Oh, my. He didn't know how right he was.

As the door drifted closed behind her, Jason's teasing fell away as he cupped her jaw and ran his thumb across her cheek. "Is this what you really want?"

She stared up at him as she let that question settle in her mind, but she already knew the answer. "I wouldn't be here if it wasn't."

He lowered his lips to hers, this time in a gentle kiss that threatened to cause her to fall for him a little more. The part of her brain that ruled self-preservation screamed at her to pull away, to get out while she still could. But the purest truth was that she didn't want to. She knew she was treading a dangerous path, but she couldn't deny what she felt for Jason any longer.

His hands trailed lightly down her arms as he gradually deepened the kiss. Then his hands gripped her waist and tugged her closer to him. She wondered how much of the heat radiating off his body was always there, and how much was being generated by the kissing, the touching, the knowing what awaited them during the night ahead.

She made a sound halfway between a moan and a whimper, which caused Jason to laugh against her lips.

"It's not wise to laugh at the woman you're hoping to get lucky with."

He brought his mouth to the side of her ear. "I'm already lucky." Then he nipped at her earlobe with his teeth.

"You're killing me," she said, breathless.

He covered her mouth with his again as his hands went to work unbuttoning her shirt. When the last button slipped free, he pushed the garment from her body and made quick work of her bra, as well.

"Your turn." She ignored the little devil sitting on her shoulder that said she should just rip his shirt open, buttons be damned. But she did get rid of his shirt as quickly as possible.

When her skin met his, a shiver overtook her body.

"Cold?" Jason wrapped his arms around her as if to keep her warm.

She shook her head. "No. It's just that..." How could she explain to him the maelstrom of emotions inside her when she couldn't even accurately define it in her own head?

One of Jason's strong hands combed through her hair to the back of her head. "We can stop if you want."

"No!"

He chuckled at her response.

"Oh, hush," she said without much force behind it.

"Gladly."

Instead of talking, he kissed her again. There was no mistaking that this kiss was different, that it was the prelude to much more. The idea of that *much more* fueled her movements, which seemed to add gasoline to the fire of his. They were naked so fast that she didn't have time to think about being embarrassed for more than a couple of seconds, but then he scooped her up into his arms and proceeded to carry her toward the bed.

"Jason, put me down before you throw out your back or something." She wasn't exactly a dainty, petite little thing.

"You do realize what I do for a living, right?"

She pressed her palm against his chest. "Are you comparing me to a steer?"

"Not at all." He dropped a kiss on her nose. "You're

a beautiful woman, and I don't want to wait another moment to get you in this bed."

He placed her atop the bed, then followed down beside her, capturing her mouth in yet another head-spinning kiss. If there were a world championship for kissing, he'd win for sure.

Although she hated the idea of him kissing anyone else. Really hated it, if she was being honest. She'd probably examine that thought later, but not now. Not when Jason's hands were exploring her body, causing her pulse to race as if it was a rocket headed to the moon.

The heat and pace of things increased with each of her breaths, which were also coming more quickly. Jason's hand skimming over her thigh just about did her in, and he must have realized it because he suddenly rolled away long enough to put on a condom. Then he was back while she was still contemplating if she'd ever breathe normally again.

Jason kissed a trail from her collarbone up to her ear. "I want you, Sloane."

"Feeling's mutual," she said, her heart beating as if she'd just climbed straight up Grand Teton without stopping.

Then he was easing her legs apart and placing himself between them. Their gazes caught and for a moment she thought she saw more in his eyes than pure desire. He maintained eye contact as he eased his way inside her.

It was Sloane who broke that eye contact when her eyes closed and she pressed her head back into her pillow as he filled her with a hot, throbbing fullness that almost made her peak before they'd even really gotten started.

Sloane's fingers dug into the muscles of Jason's back as he made love to her.

"You feel so good," he said.

She wanted to tell him the same but didn't think words existed that could adequately describe how she felt at the moment. Instead, she showed him—with her hands, her mouth, with little sounds and all of her heart.

Chapter Fourteen

The sliver of light coming through the curtains illuminated Sloane's face and the way her blond hair lay in disarray around her. He'd caused that disarray, and he had to admit that he was proud of that fact.

His body still ached for her, but he wasn't willing to wake her. She deserved her rest after driving up from Blue Falls and two rounds of enthusiastic sex. If he had his way, they'd have plenty of time to enjoy each other again after she woke.

A quick glance at the clock told him dawn wasn't far away. If she was anything like him, she was going to wake up ravenously hungry. He liked the idea of serving her breakfast in bed, so he eased out from under the cover, grabbed some clean clothes and headed for the bathroom.

The hot water felt good against his aching body. Some of it was the sweet ache that came from really good sex, but there was also the persistent ache that came from years of wrestling steers. The goal of winning the Finals was still front and center, but behind that was something he wondered if he'd just been ignoring for a while. Rodeo life wasn't as fun as it once was. If he was being honest with himself, there were some days that he dreaded heading to an arena to compete. Once there, he'd stand with his foot propped up on the pens, his arms draped across the top, and wonder what life was like for people who lived and worked in one place.

People like Sloane.

As if thinking of her conjured the reality, she slid back the shower curtain and stepped naked into the shower with him. His gaze drank in the sight of her, from her sleep-tousled hair to the breasts that made him instantly hard and all the way down her long legs.

"Well, good morning," he said, his voice rough.

Color rose in her cheeks. "Good morning."

He lifted one of his wet hands to her cheek. "You're blushing again."

"I've never done this before."

He pulled her close. "I'm glad you did, though I didn't intend to wake you up. You looked so pretty sleeping."

She laughed. "I've seen myself in the morning. *Pretty* is not the right word."

He ran his hand over her hair. "You were to me."

Sloane trailed one of her fingers along his wet biceps. "You look pretty good in the morning, too." She lifted her gaze to his, even though he got the impression it wasn't easy for her to do. "I might just have to have you for breakfast."

Red-hot desire made record time traveling from his brain to another part of his body that was more than ready for round three.

"Showering isn't what's on my mind right now."

She gave him a wicked grin. "Good."

They made love in the shower, and they weren't quiet about it. After they both reached completion, they almost slipped and fell. Sloane snorted a laugh after they prevented the crash.

"Well, that would be embarrassing, falling and breaking a bone while naked in the shower," she said.

He pulled her wet, warm body flush with his. "After that, it would be worth it."

SLOANE DIDN'T RECOGNIZE her life at the moment. After making love with Jason in the shower, he'd playfully ordered her back to bed while he went to get breakfast. She'd expected pastries and coffee from the hotel's continental spread or possibly a sausage and egg biscuit from the fast-food place across the street. What she hadn't dreamed about was him returning with two bags full of containers and a bouquet of brightly colored flowers. He was making it harder and harder to imagine having to go their separate ways soon.

"Are we expecting company?"

He lifted a brow at that, and she realized how kinky that sounded. She pointed at the bags.

"Seems like an awful lot of food for two people."

"I, for one, worked up a healthy appetite," he said as he placed the bags on the end of the bed, then leaned down to kiss her. "Plus, this way we don't have to leave for sustenance all day."

"All day?"

He grinned. "You got somewhere better to be?"

She opened her mouth to give him a teasing response. Instead, the truth came out.

"No."

He gifted her with another quick peck on the lips, then sank down beside her and began pulling out all the containers and opening them. When he was finished, a buffet of eggs, meats, pancakes, French toast and fruit lay before them.

"You bought enough to feed my entire family."

"Hardly. Remember, I've seen your brothers eat. You, too."

"Why, you..." She grabbed a pillow and swatted him with it.

He laughed before tackling her and devouring her with a kiss that almost made her forget about breakfast.

Almost.

She pushed against his chest. "You're not distracting me while all this food gets cold."

They ate as if they hadn't consumed food in a week. Good thing she'd worked off all those calories beforehand or she might not be able to fit back into her jeans after the breakfast spread.

"So you want to tell me why you ditched me last time but decided to show up here yesterday?"

She didn't immediately answer, instead taking a bite of bacon and trying to decide how honest to be. He didn't let her silence or bacon eating distract him from his question. The truth poked at the inside of her brain, demanding to be set free. Could she really tell him?

"Sloane?" Jason's voice held a note of concern.

"I like you, a lot, and that scares me."

"I scare you?"

She shook her head. "Not how you might think."

Jason stretched out on his side facing her, and she considered a quick seduction to avoid having to say more. But then he twined his fingers with hers, and as scary and mind-boggling as it was, she didn't think she'd ever felt closer to anyone.

"It's not easy for me to trust people." The rest of the truth was right there on the tip of her tongue, but she worried that speaking it would be what finally sent

Jason running for good. They were having a good time, a great time, together, but the reality was that it couldn't last. So admitting that an increasing part of her wished that it could was just setting herself up for the kind of pain she was trying desperately to avoid.

But wasn't she going to experience that pain whether or not she divulged the facts of her past?

"Someone hurt you." He didn't phrase it as a question.

She hesitated for a long moment then nodded.

"Who? I can arrange for him to get a box of horse crap in the mail."

His response was so unexpected that she barked out a laugh. "Oh, that's even better than the busted nose Ben gave him."

Jason caressed her thumb with his own, and it was insane how much that simple touch thrilled her.

"What happened?"

Sloane resisted the urge to flee, instead sinking back against her pillows. After taking a deep breath, she said, "I had a boyfriend back in high school, Blake. We were pretty serious. At least I thought so. I thought we might even get married one day, but right after we graduated I told him that I thought I was pregnant." She swallowed against the sudden, painful lump in her throat. "And this guy who I loved, who I thought loved me, told me it wasn't his problem and promptly left town."

Jason's thumb stopped caressing when his grip tightened on hers. "Crap is too good for this guy. Your brother had the right idea, although this Blake deserves more than a busted nose."

Sloane couldn't help the ill-advised surge of hope

that maybe Jason wasn't just a passing fling, that some miracle would happen and he'd surprise her by staying.

"Did you really think I could be that horrible, too?" Jason asked.

"No, but I'm not good at letting myself trust someone again. I know the deal with Blake happened a long time ago, and I know not every guy is a class-A jerk like him. Still, the last time I tried dating anyone for any length of time, let's just say that didn't improve my trust issues any. So…" People had a habit of leaving her if she cared too much. Her mother. Her father. And Blake.

Sure, she'd been surrounded by a loving family since she'd been adopted, and none of them had abandoned her. But for some reason Blake's abandonment had broken something in her, more so than she'd evidently realized.

Jason moved closer and trailed his fingers across her forehead then along her jaw. "I would never deliberately hurt you like that."

Not *deliberately*.

She shoved that distinction aside, trying not to think about it too much, as they talked about his upcoming competition schedule, the anniversary party his sister was planning for their parents and her first efforts at creating artwork with ranch animals.

"A local gallery owner wants to have a show for the paintings," she said, still not quite believing anyone in their right mind would even consider buying "artwork" made by cows and horses.

"That's great. I'll have to pull out my best jeans for that."

She chuckled at that image. "You're off the hook for the crazy art show. You'll no doubt be risking your neck in some arena with all the buckle bunnies hoping to get lucky with you."

Jason wrapped his arm around her and pulled her close to him. "You're the only buckle bunny I want. And you never know. I might just surprise you."

What did he mean? That he might show up at the art exhibit's opening? She couldn't get her hopes up that she'd even see him again after today. That was going to hurt once she left and headed home, but she flatly refused to ruin her time with him by dwelling on it now.

When he kissed her, she tasted the maple syrup he'd had on his pancakes. "You taste sweet."

"So do you."

She got the feeling he wasn't talking about syrup or the powdered sugar from the French toast.

After a round of lovemaking, during which they managed to kick several of the food containers onto the floor, she once again fell asleep in Jason's arms. When she woke, their bodies and the sheets were tangled up like strands of spaghetti. Sated, happy spaghetti. She could stay like this forever.

A casual glance toward the window revealed that the light was waning. She hadn't stepped foot outside all day, and she didn't mind. It hit her suddenly how late it was, and she shook Jason.

"Wake up. You're going to be late."

He opened his eyes a slit, barely enough to see her as he threw his arm over her naked waist. "For what?"

"The rodeo, silly. You've got to compete soon."

He surprised her by not leaping out of bed and racing for his clothes. Instead, he opened his eyes more fully and stared at her.

"What are you looking at?" She reached up, wondering if she had an award-winning case of bed head.

"Something way more appealing than wrestling a steer."

"Jason—"

"Just kiss me."

Before she could respond, his mouth plundered hers and she felt her resistance dissolve as she sank back onto the bed.

"You're going to lose all the points you'd get from this rodeo." And she knew how much his making the Finals meant to him and his family, especially his dad.

His hand skimmed down her ribs to the curve of her hip. "I'll make it up later."

She tried to protest again, but his hands and his mouth were so convincing that he'd rather stay in this hotel room with her than take another step toward his ultimate goal. She hoped he didn't regret the decision later. She hoped she didn't, because his abandoning a chance to improve his national standing made her want to believe in a commitment that most likely wasn't there. She couldn't allow herself to get her hopes up only to have them dashed.

No, she'd enjoy this weekend, and then she'd go back to her normal life. Hopefully having gotten Jason Till out of her system.

Jason still felt Sloane's lips on his, the softness of her skin beneath his fingertips, the enthusiasm of her body's response to his touch. She'd been on the road back to Blue Falls for two hours, and he couldn't get her out of his mind. He still couldn't believe he'd ditched the competition the night before, but the truth was, he didn't regret it. He'd do the same thing all over just to kiss that woman again.

He arrived at the barn where Travis had taken Jason's horse after he'd disappeared Friday night.

"Well, look who decided to grace us with his presence."

Jason looked up to see Bo smiling at him as he stood next to a couple other cowboys. "Boys, I think I finally rubbed off on Jason here. How else to explain his no-show last night? That tasty blonde, am I right?"

Jason's jaw tightened and his hands formed fists at his sides. He didn't want Bo or anyone thinking Sloane was just a weekend fling. She was so much more than that.

But what, exactly?

He didn't know the answer.

"Bo, sometimes you're a complete ass."

His friend looked taken aback at the verbal attack, but Jason didn't stick around to hear Bo's response. He hitched up his trailer, loaded his horse and drove away.

His phone rang as soon as he got on the interstate. Thinking it might be Sloane, he was surprised to hear his mother's voice on the other end of the call.

"Are you okay?" she asked.

"Yes, why?" But he suddenly realized why she was asking.

"You didn't finish the rodeo this weekend. I worried that maybe you were hurt."

"No. I just…felt like a night off." He knew that was a lame excuse as soon as he heard himself say it, but there was no taking it back. To cover up his botched explanation, he asked, "Why isn't Dad the one asking me this?"

"He's feeling a little under the weather and is sleeping."

"Is he okay?"

"Fine. Just a stomach virus that's going around."

"Is that Jason?" his father called from the background.

"You're supposed to be sleeping," his mother replied.

In the next moment, his dad was on the other extension. "Tell me you didn't miss competing because of a woman."

Jason thought about doing exactly that for about half a second before he realized how his dad's tone irritated him. "I can't do that, Dad."

"You know every single competition is imperative, right? I thought you were serious about making the Finals."

"One rodeo isn't going to make or break my chances."

"It might."

Jason bit down on an uncharacteristic angry reply. "Sorry, but I've gotta go. Getting into some heavy traffic."

Which was a lie, but it was better than going off on his dad. Especially when the man wasn't wrong. Every rodeo did count, and he did want to make the Finals. But as he gripped the steering wheel harder than necessary, he wondered if he wanted that for himself or for his dad?

As he stared at the highway in front of him, he also wondered if maybe his own dreams were changing.

Chapter Fifteen

Over the course of the next week, Jason called and texted Sloane so many times she lost count. They chatted about everything from what they were eating to her preparations for the art exhibit to how much time they'd spend in bed when they saw each other again.

That's how Jason always put it—*when*, not *if.* She was beginning to think maybe they were a couple without either of them ever actually saying it. And no matter how many times Jason texted her, she always experienced a little jolt of excitement when a new message arrived.

There was no longer any doubt in her mind. She was falling for him, and she really hoped that he felt the same. Unless she was colossally wrong, all the evidence pointed in that direction. He'd even told her more than once that he was going to make sure to attend her art exhibit opening. Even though she wasn't the artist, she had to admit the idea of the exhibit made her really nervous. It would be great to have him there beside her.

Her phone rang and she smiled, expecting it to be Jason. But when she looked at the screen, it was Elise, one of the caseworkers she worked with on the camps.

"Hey, Elise," she said in answer.

"Hi, Sloane. Do you have a minute to talk?"

"Sure. Is something wrong?"

"It's Brent Carter, one of your campers."

Cold settled in Sloane's stomach. "Has something happened to him?"

"His foster parents are moving to New York and they're giving him up."

"They're abandoning him?" The memory of the cold pain of being tossed away threatened to swallow her whole.

"I know this is out of the blue and you already do so much for these kids that I hate to ask anything more—"

"What do you need?"

"Have you ever thought about being a foster parent, or maybe even adopting a child?"

"Uh, I don't know."

"The reason I'm asking is that his foster parents said that since coming back from your camp, he's been really quiet except for when he talks about the camp, about you and about a cowboy named Jason."

Jason, who'd been the first one to tell her that he could see her adopting kids someday.

"Brent did seem to come alive while here." Of course, that was mainly with Jason, and Brent's favorite cowboy wasn't here. Would he feel just as abandoned here as where he was now?

"Normally these things take a while, but Brent has been through so many moves already. And your family has been vetted because of the camps, and the history of adoption is strong. I think we could get this expedited if you're interested."

"How long do I have to think about it?"

"Until tomorrow. I'm sorry that's so soon, but the family is moving fast on this."

"I'll let you know by tonight."

"Thanks so much. He's such a special little boy. I'd love to see him find a loving home where he could come out of his shell for good, where he'd feel safe."

Her heart ached for Brent. She knew that alone-in-the-world feeling and how it had taken a while to feel as if she was actually a part of her new family. All her brothers and sisters had been through the same thing. Even without Jason, surely they could all make Brent feel safe and loved.

But was she ready to be a mother? Until recently, she hadn't even been ready to undertake a serious romantic relationship. Motherhood was an entirely different level of commitment. But the idea of Brent being bounced around yet again made her heart ache as if it were being squeezed in a vise.

She glanced toward the house from her spot at the edge of the pasture. Before she decided anything, she needed to talk to her family.

She waited until they were all seated at dinner before she broached the subject. Ben and Neil and her sisters-in-law weren't there, but they no longer lived in their parents' house anyway.

"I need to ask you all about something," she said suddenly, drawing everyone's attention.

"This about Jason?" her mom asked, a hopeful tone in her voice.

"No." She hesitated, still unsure how to broach the subject. Maybe full steam ahead was the only reasonable option. "What would you all think of me becoming a foster parent?"

In response to the startled expressions, she launched

into a full explanation of Brent's situation, including what Elise had said about his continued attachment to life here on the ranch. She expected a ton of questions, but it seemed she'd well and truly stunned her family into silence. Surprisingly, it was her dad who spoke first.

"I think it's a great idea. You'll make a wonderful mother." That was evidently all he had to say on the matter because he proceeded to cut open his baked potato and apply butter.

"Well, it's not how I imagined you providing me with grandchildren, but you know how we feel about giving children love here, especially ones who need it the most. And it doesn't mean you can't have kids of your own, too."

Sloane had to laugh a little. Her mom wasn't going to give up on Jason becoming a member of the family, and Sloane had to admit the idea didn't bother her like it once had.

But as the meal progressed and they talked about what would happen next and how they would adjust life at the Hartley house to make a place for Brent, Sloane's thoughts kept drifting to Jason. What would he think of her decision? It wasn't as if they were so serious that he should be consulted about the decision, but she still felt as if she should give him a heads-up. But what if her suddenly having a kid changed things between them? Ended them?

She swallowed against the rising lump in her throat, hoping that wasn't the case. But if it was, she'd find a way to get over the pain. Because this time the end of the relationship would be her fault, even if she felt she was doing the right thing.

Jason smiled at the sound of Sloane's voice on the other end of the call. He wished she was as close as she sounded. Since the weekend with her in Dallas, his beds on the road had seemed mighty empty. He was beginning to think he wanted her there way more often—maybe even all the time.

There was no denying it anymore. He was falling in love with her. He thought that realization should freak him out a lot more than it did.

"Hey, beautiful," he said.

"Hey." She sounded distracted, and for some reason alarm bells started clanging like a railroad crossing in his head.

"What's wrong?"

"Nothing. Just…lots going on."

"You're always busy, but you never sound like this."

At first she didn't respond, which made him worry even more.

"I'm nervous," she said. "I'm about to make a big decision that not only affects me but also my family. And…it's going to have an effect on us."

A dark feeling formed in his chest. Instead of seeing more of her, was she about to end things with him? He'd thought she was in this as much as he was.

"I'm going to become a foster mom for Brent, maybe adopt him." She shared how he'd been uprooted over and over, and he deserved a permanent home. "I can give that to him. But if I do, I can't just take off on a weekend to meet you. And this isn't something you bargained for—"

"Sloane, stop." Yes, she'd knocked him for a loop with her news and he didn't know exactly what this meant for them, but it didn't negate that she was doing a good thing for that little boy. "You'll be a great mom."

"You think so?" She sounded unsure.

"No doubt. Brent is a lucky boy."

"Elise, his caseworker, says he mentions you a lot. His cowboy hero."

He smiled at that, but he also felt some instinct to distance himself from it. He couldn't even define his and Sloane's relationship. Neither of them had said the three little words. Bringing a kid into the picture confused things further, though he'd never say she shouldn't give Brent a home.

"Have I freaked you out enough?" she asked.

"It's a surprise, but it makes sense, too. You have a big heart."

He just wondered how much of a place he had in it.

SLOANE HATED NOT being able to see Jason's face as she dropped her bomb. He sounded supportive, but he hadn't signed up for dating a woman with a kid. But the more she thought about it, the more she realized she couldn't leave Brent to a system that treated him like the ball in a pinball machine. Even if it meant she couldn't afford to do the camps anymore.

Even if she lost the man she was pretty sure she loved.

"I have to go," she said. "Need to call Elise and make arrangements."

She wanted to ask where her decision left her and Jason, but she was too afraid of the answer.

"I hope it all goes well."

Did she hear a distance already growing in his voice, or was that her fear making her hear things that weren't there?

"Thanks. And good luck on your ride."

When they ended the call, she had to escape the house and slipped out the back door. She needed time to think and process before she called Elise. Only a couple of minutes passed before Angel caught up to her.

"You okay?"

"You mean other than I think I might have gone crazy adding motherhood to my already-busy life? Great."

Angel slipped her arm through Sloane's. "If anyone can handle it, you can."

"Why would you say that? You know firsthand how difficult being a single parent can be."

"You're perfectly capable, but I also don't think you'll be doing the parenting thing alone for long."

"You are getting way ahead of yourself. A few dates, calls and texts are one thing. Marriage and a ready-made family are something else entirely."

"You're downplaying your relationship, but you love each other."

Sloane stepped away from her sister. "Neither one of us has said that."

Angel crossed her arms. "Just because you've not said it doesn't mean it's not true."

"How could we possibly be in love? We haven't spent enough time together."

"That is just an excuse to avoid admitting a truth that scares you—that you started falling for Jason that first weekend the moment he made a connection with those kids."

"Getting along with some kids isn't the same thing as being responsible for one, being a parent."

"You're right, it's not. But it doesn't change my opinion about you and Jason. I know you, and you've never had your love for someone written so plainly on your face. Not even when you were with Blake. Definitely not Jeremy or anyone else you've gone out with."

Considering the depth of what she felt for Jason, part of her wondered if she'd even known what love was when she was with Blake. Even if she had, it had been a different kind, the love of the immature and maybe, if she was being honest, desperate to be loved. Thank goodness she was stronger now, was more of the person she was meant to be. But she knew how much it would hurt if Jason was no longer a part of her life.

"I guess time will tell if it's anything long lasting."

Angel shook her head. "Sometimes you just have to take a leap."

"I thought that's what I've been doing lately—with Jason, agreeing to an art exhibit that may be a waste of time, deciding to become a foster parent. I don't even recognize myself anymore."

"Well, from where I'm standing, the changes are positive. You deserve to be happy, and Jason makes you happier than I've ever seen you. And judging by the amount of calls and texts he sends you, that feeling goes both ways. A guy doesn't blow up his cell plan for someone who is just a booty call."

Sloane was thankful for the darkness so her sister couldn't see the way her face was burning at the memory of what had transpired in that Dallas hotel room. At the thought that she wanted it to happen again.

Angel started to turn to retrace her steps to the house, but she stopped and looked back at Sloane. "Ask yourself what you really want, more than anything, and don't let fear keep you from going after it. If you love

Jason, tell him. At least you'll know where you stand and be able to move forward accordingly."

Long after Angel went back inside, Sloane sat out on the stack of hay bales next to the pasture and stared up at the clear sky covered in stars. With each passing moment, she felt the chaos in her mind calm a bit more. As she picked out recognizable constellations, she admitted that Angel was right. Sloane loved Jason, and she needed to tell him no matter how much it frightened her.

She smiled as she let her eyes wander over Orion, letting a plan form in her mind that might change her life forever.

No MATTER HOW many times he ran the numbers, the result was always the same. He had to ride in a big rodeo this weekend in order to have a hope of making it to the Finals. On the heels of Sloane's revelation about becoming a parent, he'd not been able to focus like he should have at the last rodeo, and he'd ended up out of the money. Combined with the Dallas competition he'd ditched, he'd left himself no wiggle room.

He felt sick to his stomach—not because of how close he was cutting it but that if he hoped to salvage his season and his father's dream, it meant he'd miss Sloane's art exhibit opening. But as soon as his season was over, he'd make it up to her somehow.

Jason wasn't proud of the fact, but he put off telling her until the day before the event. They'd talked less since her big news, but he'd attributed that to how busy she was. He supposed it was at least partially because he didn't know what to say.

But he wasn't willing to just stand her up on her big night, one that might determine the future of her camps.

He ran his hand over his face when it hit him that he was putting his goals above hers. He honestly didn't know if his decision would be the same were it not that his dad wanted to see him win the Finals so much. It seemed the man thought of little else. And his parents had been so supportive of him throughout his entire life, how could he deny his father this one wish?

Still, he felt as if he might throw up as he placed the call to Sloane. It took four rings before she answered. One more and it would have gone to voice mail. The fact that he knew that told him just how many times he'd called her, how much he liked hearing the sound of her voice instead of just reading her words in a text message.

"You sound out of breath," he said.

"That's because I'm running around like a balloon animal fleeing a porcupine. Every time I turn my back, I feel as if my to-do list gets busy making more items."

"You have to watch those to-do lists. They're known for being frisky."

"Great, now you tell me." She pulled the phone away from her mouth to say something to someone else. "Sorry."

"No problem. Should I call back?" Damn it, why did he ask that? He needed to get to the reason for his call and get it over with.

"No. In fact, I'm going to actually sit down and relax while I talk to you."

He hated himself even more because she wasn't going to be relaxing for long.

"So what time do you think you'll be here tomorrow?" she asked.

He closed his eyes for a moment and asked for divine help in breaking the news as gently as possible.

"I can't make it." So much for divine intervention.

"What?"

"I'm so sorry, Sloane, but I have to compete this weekend. No way I'll make the Finals if I don't. Not after the way I flubbed up last weekend." He wasn't about to mention the failure to complete the Dallas rodeo. He didn't want her thinking he blamed her.

"Oh."

"I wish I could compete closer so I could do both, but there's nothing—"

"You don't have to explain. I understand."

From the sound of her voice, he wasn't so sure about that. He wasn't an expert or anything, but he'd swear she sounded as if she was hurt but trying to hide it.

"I'll make it up to you."

"There's no need. You've been working toward this all year. It's more important than looking at silly paintings by cows and horses."

"They're not silly. This exhibit will help get you closer to your goal, too."

"We'll see."

He hated how doubtful she sounded and wished more than anything that he could pull her into his arms, make her believe that everything was going to be okay.

They talked a few minutes longer, but then she said she had to get back to work. As usual, she wished him good luck. But for the first time, he wasn't sure if she meant it.

SLOANE WALKED AWAY from the cluster of people she'd been talking to for the past few minutes because she was afraid her fake smile was going to start crumbling. She walked toward the front of the gallery and perused the series of pictures of past campers, photos of laughter and smiles captured by Angel's camera. Sloane was afraid there would be no more laughter and smiles to capture because the opening was almost over and only one painting had sold, to a tourist from Denver.

It was as if the universe was twisting the dagger in her middle just a little more. Not only was the opening going poorly, but she'd been abandoned once again. And where was Jason competing tonight? Denver.

She knew the reason he'd given her was perfectly valid. She'd checked out the standings herself because she was evidently a glutton for punishment, but her investigation had shown the truth of his words. If he didn't compete and do well this weekend, his dream of getting back to the Finals and having a chance to finally win was over. At least for this year.

Still, she couldn't help the pain consuming her middle. And it was ten times worse than when Blake had left her. So maybe Jason hadn't technically left her, but her gut told her it was only a matter of time. Doubts had begun pecking at her the moment she'd told him about Brent. His decision to skip the opening, even though part of her totally understood why, just added to those doubts. She needed to end things first because she was bringing Brent home soon, and there was no way she was going to get his hopes up about Jason being a part of his life and then have Jason break Brent's little heart. He'd been through too much already. She'd find a way to navigate her own loss, but she'd do everything in her power to protect Brent. Even pushing away the man she loved.

"I love looking at all those darling faces."

Sloane glanced over at Merline Teague, owner of the gallery. "Yeah, they're special kids."

"Is something wrong, honey? You sound sad."

Sloane managed a smile she hoped was convincing. "Just tired."

"And you were hoping to sell more paintings tonight."

"I shouldn't have. I mean, they're not really art, after all."

"Art is in the eye of the beholder. Personally, I think your livestock are way more talented than some famous painters."

Sloane appreciated Merline's words of support, but she was still faced with the fact that at the very least she was going to need to postpone any future camps. She needed to focus her time, energy and money on Brent.

Merline turned to leave, then placed her hand on Sloane's forearm. "Don't be too disheartened. Things have a way of working out in the end."

Sloane got the feeling that it wasn't only the paintings and camps she was talking about. She had hoped no one in her family would mention Jason's absence, but maybe someone had let it slip. Or perhaps Merline was just speaking from experience. After all, she had three sons of her own, all of whom were happily married now, but not before going through some serious ups and downs in their relationships.

After the opening finally ended, Sloane made sure to thank everyone for attending before she gave Merline a quick hug and practically raced to her truck, thankful she'd arrived earlier and separate from the rest of her family. As soon as she sat in the driver's seat, her phone rang.

When she saw it was Jason, she didn't answer. She wasn't ready to talk to him yet because she didn't know what she was going to say, or even if she could get through it without crying the way she had after he'd told her he wasn't going to be at the art exhibit opening.

She'd promised herself years ago she wasn't ever going to let a man make her cry again, but she hadn't been able to stop the tears.

When she didn't answer, it didn't take long for a text message to come in. Unable to keep herself from looking, she read it.

Hope the opening went well and you sold tons of paintings for tons of money.

Her thumbs hovered above the screen, but she decided not to respond. If she was going to end things, there was no need to seem hasty to reply. With another of those annoying lumps forming in her throat, she tossed the phone aside and headed home.

As soon as she reached the house, she took advantage of the fact that she was the first one there and went straight to her room. She didn't even turn on the light, hoping they'd think she was so tired she'd gone to bed. The truth was she was tired, in more ways than one.

She heard her phone buzz again, and she suspected Jason might continue to text until he heard from her. Blinking back tears, she retrieved her phone and typed a response to his first message without even reading the newest one.

Went fine. Really tired. Going to bed now.

And that's exactly what she did, trying not to think about Jason lying in a bed hundreds of miles away. Trying but failing to avoid wishing he was lying beside her instead. As she curled up beneath the covers, her plush giraffe wrapped in her arms, she lost the battle once again as tears leaked from her eyes to soak her pillow.

Chapter Sixteen

Jason laughed at what must have been a funny story told by his brother-in-law, even though he had no clue what Kevin had said. He just took his cue from the other people standing around the same circle.

Ever since he'd gotten the short, emotionless text from Sloane after the art exhibit opening, he'd had a hard time concentrating on anything. He'd darn near skipped his parents' anniversary party to drive to Texas. It didn't take a genius to figure out that he'd hurt her even though she'd said she understood. Did she think he was abandoning her the way her scumbag of an ex had? The way she felt so many people in her life had, whether it had been their choice or not?

"Can I steal you?" Shannon asked as she slipped her arm through his. She didn't wait for an answer before turning him away from the others and escorting him straight out the back door.

Thankfully it was one of the warmer November days in Idaho. This time of year, it could go from pleasant to frigid within hours.

"What's up?" he asked.

"Not your mood. What happened?"

"Nothing. I'm fine."

"You forget I've been sniffing out your lies since you were born. Is this about Sloane?"

"What makes you say that?"

"Well, maybe the fact that every time we talk, you spend more time talking about her than rodeo, and today you haven't mentioned her once."

He gestured toward the house with his thumb. "This is Mom and Dad's day."

"Don't you think it would make them happy that you've finally found someone?"

"Not according to Dad."

Shannon's look of surprise was so genuine it made him wish he hadn't introduced that bit of info into the conversation. "Tell me what he said."

"It doesn't matter. I think Sloane is done with me."

"Why do you say that?"

"I don't want to talk about this."

"Tough. You're not going back in that house until you spill even if I have to tackle you by the ankles and hold you here."

He had no doubt she wouldn't hesitate to do exactly that. With a sigh, he walked over to the wooden swing hanging from a frame that faced out toward the snow-capped mountains in the distance and sat. Then he told her about how their dad didn't want a woman distracting him from the goal of making the Finals, how he'd had to bail on Sloane to keep the possibility of reaching that goal alive. And about how he felt as if Sloane was pulling away because of it.

"You do know that it's your life and not Dad's, right? He had his chance."

"But he should have had more chances."

"It's not your fault that he didn't."

"She's right."

Jason turned toward the sound of his mother's voice. She walked toward where he and Shannon sat and sank onto the bench next to the swing.

"You need to do what makes you happy."

"I am," he said.

"Your heart hasn't been in riding for a while."

"What? Of course it has." The dream of winning the Finals wasn't his dad's dream alone. But was that dream as strong as it once was?

His mom reached over and squeezed his hand. "You love Sloane, don't you?"

"I don't know."

His mom smiled at the same time Shannon made a frustrated sound. "Yes, you do. You need to tell her that."

Jason didn't even wait until the party was over to call Sloane. But again, she didn't answer. Well, he wasn't accepting her silence, not without laying out all his feelings. He wasn't sure what he was going to do about the rest of the rodeo season yet, but he did know that he had to speak to Sloane, so he called the Hartleys' house number.

Angel was the one to answer the phone. "Oh, hi. Sloane's not here."

His frustration level rose at the same time as his heart sank. "She's not answering her phone."

Angel's lack of a quick explanation made him wonder if he'd already missed his chance.

"Please tell me she doesn't think I abandoned her."

"Jason, I'm sorry. She understood, but I think it made her believe that she should end things. She says she's protecting Brent from any possible heartbreak, but I know my sister. That's only part of the reason."

"This has to do with Blake." Again, he wanted to find her ex and punish him for hurting Sloane.

But he'd done the same thing, hadn't he? Not intentionally, but sometimes actions had unintended consequences.

"Yeah. She thinks by being the one to leave the relationship first, she'll be protecting herself from worse hurt when you inevitably leave her."

"I would never do that. I love her."

"I know."

"You do?"

"Yes. But don't worry. It's usually obvious to onlookers way before the people actually involved."

"Does—" He stopped himself from asking the question when he realized how desperate it sounded.

"Yes, but it doesn't matter at this point."

Doesn't matter? "I don't understand."

"Sloane has to come to big changes in her life in her own time without pressure, no matter how much we might try to convince her otherwise."

He wasn't sure that was true. "She seemed to decide to become a foster parent pretty quickly."

"Not really. That was going to happen eventually, even if she didn't realize it. Every time she'd hold a camp, those kids took a piece of her heart with them. She'd adopt every kid in foster care, every orphan if she could."

Angel was right. He'd told Sloane something similar himself, and he'd seen with his own eyes how much watching the campers being driven away from the ranch had affected her.

"It'll hurt her if she can't hold the camps anymore,

but at least she'll be giving a little boy a real home and lots of love," Angel said.

"She's not having any more camps?"

"We don't know yet. She's trying to think of more fund-raising ideas, but it's on the back burner at the moment."

"What about the art sales?"

Angel sighed. "Not going well. She only sold one small piece at the opening and none since."

His heart fell like a stone into the pit of his stomach. Not only had the opening not gone well, but he also hadn't been there to support her.

"What should I do?"

"I know this isn't the answer you want and it's counterintuitive, but give her time. I have faith she'll come around when she's ready."

Angel was right. That wasn't the answer he wanted. He'd give Sloane time, but he couldn't just wait and do nothing. He was going to make things right—for everyone. His parents. Sloane. And himself.

The first step was talking to his dad. Unwilling to put a damper on the anniversary celebrations, however, he decided to wait until the next day. When his dad found him in the barn later that night, Jason took the opportunity before he chickened out.

"What's on your mind, son? You look as if your thoughts are a million miles away."

Actually, a little over fourteen hundred miles, but who was counting?

"Been thinking about the Finals."

"You seem to be back on track. You're going to make it. I feel it in my old, creaky bones."

"That's the plan." With a deep breath, he turned toward his dad. "I'm going to do my best to win, but after it's done I'm retiring."

"You sure that's what you want?"

That hadn't been the reaction Jason expected. He'd pictured his dad trying to talk him out of it, telling him he still had some good years left in him. Had his mom said something to his dad?

"Yes."

"You've found the one, haven't you?"

Jason smiled. His dad wasn't the most romantic of men, but there'd never been any doubt about Jason's mom being the one and only woman for his dad.

"Yeah, I have. I just have to convince her." Though they'd never really talked about feelings before, Jason found himself filling his dad in on the situation with Sloane.

His dad nodded as if he understood perfectly. "Being adopted, you always feel as if relationships are temporary, as if they might disappear in the blink of an eye. And sounds as if her jackass of an ex didn't help matters any."

He'd never known his dad felt that way, but that was no surprise, what with the whole not talking about feelings thing.

"No, he didn't. Good thing I don't know where he is."

His dad chuckled a bit at that. "Yeah, good thing. Can't make it to the Finals if you're sitting in jail for assault."

And he'd be spending his time more constructively by helping Sloane get past the...well, the past.

"What are you going to do once you retire?"

"I have no idea. But I plan to do it in Texas."

Where Sloane would hopefully be at his side. And where he could help her make her dream come true.

SLOANE MADE SURE to smile at Brent every time he looked at her, wanting him to feel loved and as if his new home had been his home his entire life. Her heart lifted as the members of her family took turns engaging Brent. Her mother promised him chocolate cake the next day. Julia said she would lend him her favorite puzzle. Neil said he'd take him on a ride around the ranch. Ben made Brent giggle when he put a dollop of mashed potatoes on the end of his nose. She'd worried when she picked up Brent because he'd been really quiet, had retreated back into his shell.

But a couple of days at the ranch and he was like a different kid. She could still see the worry in his eyes sometimes, as if he was afraid he was dreaming and would wake up at any moment, but at least he was laughing now, speaking more and more with the people around him.

Her heart filled with more happiness than she had dared hope she'd ever feel again. Even so, there was still a spot that remained empty and lonely. But she'd made the right choice. She hadn't had a text or call from Jason in two weeks. It hurt, hurt a lot, but at least she'd ended things before she'd revealed exactly how she felt about him. Feelings she would have to find a way to eliminate from her heart.

"He looks happy," Angel said from her seat next to Sloane.

"He does, doesn't he?"

"I only wish his mom was half as happy."

She knew Angel thought she'd made a big mistake cutting things off with Jason, but she had more to consider now than her own feelings. It probably seemed irrational to everyone around her, but she couldn't stand the idea of Brent being abandoned one more time. A voice in her head told her she was inventing an eventuality that wasn't there. Jason had surprised her with how attentive he was, how caring, how loving, even when he was hundreds of miles away.

But he'd never said he loved her. To be fair, she hadn't admitted her feelings either. Those feelings aside, realistically how long could they keep going like they had been? Didn't absence make hearts grow fonder only if those hearts eventually were going to be living in the same place?

She'd gotten so lost in her thoughts that she realized too much time had passed to respond to Angel. Her sister had already directed her attention to a conversation with Mandy. Even with her entire family surrounding her, Sloane suddenly felt incredibly alone.

After dinner and a family viewing of *A Christmas Story*, Sloane scooped up Brent, who had fallen asleep in her father's lap, and carried him to bed. Not wanting to wake him, she decided to forgo changing him into his little reindeer pajamas. She slipped off his sneakers and pulled the covers over him.

For a few moments, she sat on the side of his bed in what had once been Ben's room and simply watched him sleep, grateful he felt safe enough to do so. Hoping she didn't wake him up, she reached over and gave him a light kiss before easing out of the room.

After stopping by the kitchen for a couple of snickerdoodles Mandy's mom had sent over in a big tin, she headed back to the living room.

"What are you all watching?" Sloane asked as she entered the room.

But then she heard the words *National Finals Rodeo* on the TV and turned to look at the screen. She froze as she saw a steer wrestler race out of the chute in hot pursuit of the released steer. It wasn't Jason, but she knew he was there. Despite her determination not to communicate with him, she hadn't been strong enough to stop checking the standings right up until she saw that he'd made the Finals.

"We want to see Jason compete," her mom said.

Sloane suspected that was only half true. The other half of the reason had to do with her family's belief that she'd made a mistake avoiding him until he'd disappeared from her life.

She should just go to her room, but the draw of seeing him, even if on a TV screen, was too strong.

They all watched as two more steer wrestlers made their runs, garnering really good scores. Of course, the level of competition was much higher at the Finals than at the local rodeos. In Vegas, everyone was a potential champion, the cream of the rodeo crop.

Her heart started thumping harder when she saw Jason was up next. She suspected at least some of her family members were watching for her reaction, but she kept her eyes focused on the screen as Jason and his hazer got into position.

"Next up is Idaho cowboy Jason Till," the announcer said. "Till has been here once before, and he's no doubt hoping to improve on his first appearance."

Sloane felt as if everything slipped into slow motion except the frantic beating of her heart. The screen showed a close-up of Jason's face, and she missed him so much she thought her heart would actually break to pieces. She watched as he nodded, and then the race against the clock was on. She held her breath as Jason started leaning off the side of his horse and then went sailing through the air.

The steer was an ornery one, but Jason finally got the animal flipped and tied. But then the animal jerked its head right as Jason appeared to trip. She gasped at the same time as the crowd on TV.

"Looks like Till may have just taken a horn to the face." The camera focused on Jason long enough for her to see the blood pouring from his cheek right below his eye before cutting away.

"Oh, my God," she said, as her mother, who was sitting on the end of the couch nearest Sloane, gripped her hand.

It was then that Sloane realized she was shaking uncontrollably. As scared as she was, she couldn't tear her gaze away from the TV. She wanted to be there to help him, to make sure he was taken care of.

She wasn't sure how long it actually was but it felt like an eternity before Jason got to his feet with the help of a couple of other cowboys. She couldn't tell how bad the injury was because the camera angles were such that viewers weren't exposed to the gruesome cut.

"Look there, honey," her mom said. "He's walking out under his own power."

Right as her mom finished speaking, Jason lifted an arm and waved to the crowd. But Sloane could tell from the slowness of his movements that he was in pain.

When the coverage cut to a commercial for pickup trucks, Sloane felt as if she was going to be ill. Her mom squeezed her hand again, drawing her attention.

"Honey, you need to go to him."

Sloane shook her head, even though she wanted nothing more than to run straight to Jason and beg him to forgive her for ruining the best thing that had ever happened to her.

"I can't. I just brought Brent home."

"And he'll be fine with us."

"I don't want him to feel as if I'm abandoning him."

"He'll understand you'll be back, and we'll keep him busy and safe."

Sloane stood and paced to the side of the room. "It's too expensive to travel."

"I have a ton of unused frequent flier miles you're welcome to use," Arden said.

"And we'll all chip in for the rest of the expenses," Neil added.

Sloane scanned the faces of her family and realized once again just how lucky she was that she'd been adopted into the Hartley clan.

"Why are you all doing this?"

"Because we love you, and you love that boy," her father said. "Pretty damn sure he loves you, too."

How could her dad possibly know that?

"He does," Angel said. "He told me so."

Sloane stared in disbelief at her sister. "He told you? He never said that to me."

"I told him to hold off because you weren't ready to hear it."

Sloane started to speak but Angel stopped her.

"You had to be ready to reciprocate, and you weren't ready. Now you are."

They all seemed so sure. Could she let down her guard enough to trust they were right?

"Okay."

She was going to Vegas.

Chapter Seventeen

Jason's face hurt as if the Devil had lanced him with his pitchfork. But at least he still had his eye. If that steer's horn had hit him a fraction higher, he might not have been so lucky.

He popped a couple of ibuprofen while dreading the idea of jumping off a horse and wrestling another steer. But he didn't have a choice. He could grit through the pain, and then hang it up knowing that he'd done his best, however this week turned out.

When he arrived at the arena, he received a couple of friendly pats on the back from fellow competitors, a few comments about how lucky he'd been and some best wishes for that night's competition. This was it, the final night. The time he received tonight would determine where he ended up. No pressure or anything.

As they often did, his thoughts went to Sloane. He missed her and wished that she could be here on his big night.

Angel had texted him good luck from the entire family, but he doubted Sloane knew about the message. He didn't think she wished him ill, might even still be rooting for him to win—but from a safe distance. If things went his way tonight, he'd have what he needed when he went back to Blue Falls to tell Sloane he loved her and that from now on he'd be there for her whenever she needed him, if she'd give him the chance.

But now wasn't the time to think about that big step in his life. There was one that needed to come before it, and it was going to require the ride of his life. He scanned the arena, how it was filling up. Someone wildly gesturing with her arms drew his attention, and his heart nearly stopped. He blinked a couple of times, thinking he was seeing things that weren't there. But she was still standing by the boards, still waving to get his attention.

Sloane.

He climbed and leaped over the gate and headed straight for her. When he got close, he stopped a few feet short, still not quite trusting his eyes.

"Hey," she said, sounding nervous.

"How are you here?"

"One airplane flight and a harrowing taxi ride through Vegas traffic."

"Why?"

She swallowed visibly, then pointed toward the bandage on his face. "I saw it happen, and I've never been so scared in my life."

"I'm okay. You didn't have to come all the way out here."

"Yes, I did." She took a couple of steps toward him. "I had to tell you how I feel, ask you to forgive me for being a fool."

"That sounds a lot like what I was going to say when I came back to ask you to give me another chance."

The change in her expression gave him hope, so he said what had been aching to come out for a while. But he'd needed to say it in person, and now here she stood right in front of him.

"I love you, Sloane. I know you were told that before and were done wrong, but I swear to you I'll never leave again."

She smiled and her eyes took on a new glow, but he also still detected a touch of sadness.

"I love you, too, but please don't promise that. You'll have to leave to compete, and I understand—"

He closed the rest of the distance between them and dropped his mouth to hers. He'd startled her, but it only took a breath for her to sink into the kiss and wrap her arms around his neck. Somewhere beyond the bubble of happiness enveloping him, he heard a few appreciative whistles.

He broke the kiss but still held her close.

"This is my last rodeo. I'm retiring after tonight."

"You are? Wait, you don't have to do that on my account."

"It's for me, too. I don't feel the same passion for it anymore. There are other things I want more." He dropped a light kiss on her lips. "And you, Sloane Hartley, are at the top of that list...if you'll have me."

"Well, it would have been stupid for me to come all this way just to say no."

"True. But I do have one more ride, and I'm feeling pretty good about it now."

In fact, as he walked back toward the end of the arena, he felt as if he was ten feet tall and walking on air.

SLOANE WATCHED JASON walk away, wanting to run after him and tell him not to ride. The memory of seeing him injured on TV would not let her rest, and she thought watching him ride live might make her ill. But he had to get through only one more ride, and then he was done. She still couldn't believe it. Even with no idea what the future might hold for them, excitement danced through her at the possibilities.

"Sloane?"

She turned at the sound of her name to see a lovely woman who seemed somehow familiar. Then it clicked. "Shannon?"

The other woman smiled. "I hoped that was you. Otherwise, I was going to be really confused why my brother was kissing a random woman in front of an arena full of people."

Sloane's face heated. "I...I wasn't expecting that."

Shannon laughed. "He's been saving up. Come on, sit with us. There are two seats next to us that no one has claimed all week."

Us? Oh, Lord, she was about to meet Jason's family. The family who'd just seen them kissing as if they'd been somewhere private.

All the world's butterflies seemed to have suddenly migrated to her stomach as she accompanied Shannon up the steps. She picked out Jason's mom when they were still several steps away. The huge smile was a dead giveaway.

"You must be Sloane," the older woman said as they reached her.

"Yes, ma'am."

Mrs. Till pulled Sloane into a big hug as if she'd known her all her life. Shannon introduced her father, husband and children, Jason's twin niece and nephew.

"I've heard a lot about you all." Sloane really wanted to sit down before her legs failed her.

"And we've heard about you," Mrs. Till said in that way that told Sloane she approved.

Sloane was surprised by how relieved she felt. And as she finally sat and began getting to know Jason's family, she relaxed gradually. By the time the rodeo started, she no longer felt nervous. At least not about Jason's family. His ride was another story. Thank goodness steer wrestling was the second event. If Jason were a bull rider, the last event on the schedule, she didn't think she could bear it.

Jason's dad must have sensed her anxiety because he gripped her hand in support. She smiled at the older man, thinking that this was what Jason would look like in a couple of decades. She sure hoped she was there beside him as they aged.

She made it through the bareback event, then what felt like countless steer wrestlers before it was finally Jason's turn. As Jason and his hazer got into position, she gripped Mr. Till's hand even harder.

"Don't worry. He's got this," his dad said. "It's his year."

She hoped he was right, but it didn't allow her stomach to relax one iota. All the buildup to something that barely lasted the blink of an eye. The nod, the steer breaking the barrier, Jason and his hazer racing forward, Jason leaning out of the saddle and grabbing those dangerous horns and wrestling the steer to its side—it all happened so fast. When Jason threw his hands up in the air, the announcer said, "Ladies and gentleman, you just witnessed a world-record time!"

Sloane jumped to her feet screaming and cheering along with the rest of the arena. Happiness for Jason flooded her, but it wasn't over yet. There were still two more riders to go. Her nervousness returned full force. Jason was so close to achieving his dream. He just couldn't have it snatched away now.

The next rider's time put him in fifth place. As the final rider backed into the chute, Sloane felt as if everyone in the arena was holding a collective breath. The guy's time was fast, but not fast enough.

Jason had won. He was the new world champion.

Sloane jumped up and down and proceeded to hug the entire Till family. They were still celebrating when suddenly Jason was there, too. He must have raced to her side, and he wasted no time kissing her.

"You did it," she said when he pulled away. "You achieved your dream."

"Which means you'll be achieving yours, too."

She grinned at him. "Thinking highly of yourself again, I see."

"Not me. This win comes with a nice check, plenty for you to fund camps for the foreseeable future."

She was so stunned she didn't know what to say. When she finally found her voice, she said, "You can't do that. It's your money."

"To do with as I please. And it pleases me to help the woman I love give a lot of kids who deserve it a little time away."

Tears pooled in her eyes. "I love you."

"Love you more," he said with the same grin he'd given her outside the arena in Blue Falls that first night.

Finally, she believed they'd have a lifetime of arguing over who loved the other more. That was the type of argument she could live with.

* * * * *

If you loved this book, look for more in
Trish Milburn's BLUE FALLS, TEXAS *series:*

HOME ON THE RANCH
A RANCHER TO LOVE
THE COWBOY TAKES A WIFE
IN THE RANCHER'S ARMS
THE RANCHER'S SURPRISE BABY

Available now from Harlequin Western Romance!

SPECIAL EXCERPT FROM

⊕ HARLEQUIN®

Western Romance

*Cole McCullough must find the birth mother of the
twin babies left outside his door. When his ex-girlfriend
Stacy Rowe offers to help, he's in for much more than he
bargained for!*

*Read on for a sneak preview of
the next heartwarming installment of the*
FOREVER, TEXAS *series,*
TWINS ON THE DOORSTEP,
by USA TODAY *bestselling author Marie Ferrarella!*

"You really found these babies on your doorstep?" Stacy
asked several minutes later.

She had gotten into the back seat of his truck and he had
handed her the wicker basket with the babies. The infants
were dozing and the silence in the truck felt overwhelming.
Stacy couldn't think of anything else to say, and every
other topic would set them off on a course she had no
desire to travel.

"Yes, I did," he answered, getting into the driver's seat.
He glanced at her over his shoulder.

As if she didn't know where he'd found the babies, he
thought.

He was staring at her, Stacy realized, and it took
everything she had not to squirm in her seat. This was a
totally bad idea, going with Cole to the clinic like this. But
no one said no to Miss Joan, and Stacy wasn't about to be
the first. She had no desire to have her head handed to her.

"Do you have any idea who the mother might be?" Stacy asked him.

Okay, Cole thought, he'd play along. "There might be a few possibilities," he responded vaguely. "But that's why I came with them to Miss Joan. She's always on top of everything and I figure that she'd be the first to know whose babies they were."

"Miss Joan doesn't know everything," Stacy insisted.

"Maybe," he agreed. "But right now, I figured she was my best shot."

Why are we playing these games, Stacy? Tell me the truth. Are these babies mine?

For one moment, he wrestled with an overwhelming desire to ask the woman in the back seat just that. It would explain why she'd left town so abruptly. But he knew asking her was pointless. He knew her. She wouldn't answer him. In all likelihood, she'd just walk out on him the way she had the last time.

And, angry as he was about her leaving him, he didn't want that happening again. Not until he'd had a chance to talk with her—*really* talk.

Don't miss TWINS ON THE DOORSTEP
by Marie Ferrarella, available October 2017
wherever Harlequin® Western Romance books
and ebooks are sold.

www.Harlequin.com

Looking for more satisfying love stories
with community and family at their core?

Check out **Harlequin® Special Edition**
and **Harlequin® Western Romance** books!

New books available every month!

CONNECT WITH US AT:

Harlequin.com/Community

Facebook.com/HarlequinBooks

Twitter.com/HarlequinBooks

Instagram.com/HarlequinBooks

Pinterest.com/HarlequinBooks

ReaderService.com

**ROMANCE WHEN
YOU NEED IT**

HFGENRE2017R

LOVE
Harlequin
romance?

Join our Harlequin community to share your
thoughts and connect with other
romance readers!

Be the first to find out about promotions,
news, and exclusive content!

Sign up for the Harlequin e-newsletter and
download a free book from any series at

www.TryHarlequin.com

CONNECT WITH US AT:

Harlequin.com/Community

 Facebook.com/HarlequinBooks

 Twitter.com/HarlequinBooks

 Instagram.com/HarlequinBooks

 Pinterest.com/HarlequinBooks

ReaderService.com

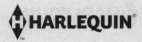 **HARLEQUIN**®

**ROMANCE WHEN
YOU NEED IT**

HSOCIAL2017

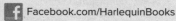

Looking for inspiration in tales
of hope, faith and heartfelt romance?

Check out **Love Inspired**®,
Love Inspired® **Suspense** and
Love Inspired® **Historical** books!

New books available every month!

CONNECT WITH US AT:

www.LoveInspired.com

Harlequin.com/Community

www.ReaderService.com

Love Inspired®

LIGENRE2017